"Canada!" I stared at them. "But that's thousands of miles away!"

"There's no war in Canada," Dad said. "Ye'll be safe there."

"I don't want to be safe. I want to stay here with you."

"It's lucky we are to get ye on the ship, so it is," Dad said. "There's hundreds on the Seavac waiting list. The ship was full, but then a couple canceled. It's the grand piece of luck right enough. They sail tomorrow, the twelfth."

"But *Canada*!" I was practically speechless. I hated them. They might just as well have said the moon. What did I know of Canada! Nothing, except it was very large, was colored red on the map, and was the white, frozen part of North America. I'd be alone. Alone on a ship. Alone in a strange country. My mam and dad hated me and I hated them. They wanted rid of me. I could feel my eyes start to well with tears.

My mam reached out, but I flung myself away, and thumped up the stairs.

WISH ME LUCK

James Heneghan

LAUREL-LEAF
BOOKS

Published by
Bantam Doubleday Dell Books for Young Readers
a division of
Bantam Doubleday Dell Publishing Group, Inc.
1540 Broadway
New York, New York 10036

Visit us on the Web! www.bdd.com

Educators and librarians, visit the BDD Teacher's
Resource Center at www.bdd.com/teachers

ISBN: 0-440-22764-X

RL: 5.1

Reprinted by arrangement with Farrar, Straus and Giroux

Printed in the United States of America

November 1998

10 9 8 7 6 5 4 3 2 1

OPM

For Lucy

WISH ME LUCK

ONE

We made fun of him right from the start.

Behind his back.

We didn't dare do it to his face because he looked tough and mean. He looked dangerous.

He had black hair, uncombed and dirty, cut by his mam with the potato peeler, it looked like. He had a black eye that he must have got in a fight, and a scowl like a wild boar's. Instead of a school uniform he wore a man's jacket that was half of a scruffy old blue pinstripe suit, much too big for him, with sagging shoulders where the padding had slipped, and shiny snot marks on the sleeves. His shoes, too, were a couple of sizes too big, with string instead of laces.

But he had a certain swagger.

Nobody wanted to be the first to start anything with him, not even Stinky Corcoran, who was the best fighter in the whole school.

But we mocked him behind his back, the way boys do when they're a bit scared. At first we made fun of his scruffy appearance and his lack of a uniform—gray trousers, cap and blazer in navy and royal blue, with the school motto, *Semper Fidelis,* emblazoned on the cap and on the blazer pocket in gold. Then it was his foreignness, his accent. "Dayn" instead of "down," and "hayss" instead of "house." Mainly, though, it was the way he acted so tough. "It's no wonder he's got a black eye," said a boy called Two-Ply.

"Struts about like a landlord," agreed my friend Bren.

He had come to Liverpool from Northern Ireland so his dad could try to find work in the munitions factory.

He lived next door to me.

His name was Tom Bleeker, and he was the new kid at Snozzy's at the beginning of September. Snozzy's was St. Oswald's School.

The war was just one year old.

American gangster movies were popular, in spite of the war. So because of the way Bleeker acted so tough, some of the kids started calling him Mr. Big behind his back.

But he wasn't big. He was about my size, which was about normal for a thirteen-year-old. If anything, he was a bit on the skinny side if you ask me.

Another thing the kids found funny was the sight of tough Mr. Big walking to and from school with his little sister, Elsie, who was a tiny bit of a thing in her first year in Infants, hair cut with the bread knife. She was usually slightly behind him, whining, trying hard to keep up. Whenever she fell too far behind, Bleeker yelled at her,

4

"Move yer legs, worm! Move yer legs!" in that funny tight-voweled accent of his so that "legs" came out as "ligs" and "worm" as "wurrim."

"Don't you have no mam to take you to school?" the kids asked the little girl.

If she slowed to answer, Bleeker would shout back, "Take no notice of them yahoos!" Then he'd grab her by the wrist and yank her along.

"Is your mam so ugly she can't come out in the daylight?" the kids shouted after them, goading him to see if he'd fight.

Bleeker scowled and looked like he wanted to kill them.

Because he was the same age as me, we were in the same class, Miss O'Hara's, along with my three pals, Charlie McCauley, Bren O'Dougherty, and Gordie Darwin.

The biggest kid in the class, and the whole school, was Stinky Corcoran, who stood out like a gorilla on a chicken farm. He had been left back for two years, and was probably about fifteen.

As we got bolder and started making fun of Bleeker's accent, and calling him Mr. Big to his face, we looked to Stinky Corcoran for some action. "Bleeker walks about like he owns the place," we complained to Stinky. "He says he can beat anyone. Black his other eye for him," we suggested.

But Stinky Corcoran, slow to anger, merely regarded us suspiciously through his tiny eyes, red like marbles.

Except for war propaganda and a few bombs on the docks, the Germans had done practically nothing to Liverpool for a whole year, and in our Old Swan district we wouldn't have known there was a war on at all if it wasn't for the noisy air-raid siren tests and the sight of the little kids carrying their gas masks with them everywhere they went, so a few kids started a propaganda war of their own: "You're not scared of the new kid, are you, Stinky?" they said. "Bleeker says you're ugly and stupid. Are you gonna let him get away with that?"

Stinky began to eye the new kid suspiciously.

The fight took place right after school. In the glassy blue air of late summer, with hardly a cloud in the sky, the day was perfect. It was the first fight of the year. All of us boys wanted it, for it would be a proper start to the new school year, an initiation ceremony, a way of getting things rolling. You couldn't depend on the Germans for excitement. There had been wild bombing raids on Fighter Command bases in the south and southeast areas of England, and on the City of London, but for us in Old Swan, the war was only a distant rumble, a non-starter. It was like a football match when the other side forgets to turn up.

We all followed Stinky and Bleeker down to the Albany Street playground, searching the sky as we went along for a Hurricane or a Spitfire, or a German reconnaissance plane that might have sneaked through without the alert sirens going off. That was all we ever saw in Liverpool, if we were lucky, one pencil-thin Dornier, taking photographs of the docks or, more likely, lost and trying to find its way back south and over the English Channel.

Bleeker ordered his sister to go on home. It was only two streets away.

Bleeker and Stinky peeled off their jackets and threw them on top of the monkey bars. Neither one of them wanted to fight, not really. Their hearts weren't in it, we could all see that. They were going through the motions only because it was expected of them, and because they wanted to have it over and done with.

They stood and eyed each other, rolling up their already rolled-up shirtsleeves. They squared off, fists raised.

"This is ridiculous," said Gordie. "Bleeker's only half the size of Stinky Corcoran."

"He'll be slaughtered," I agreed.

"Killed," sighed Bren.

"Murdered," said Charlie happily.

That was what we all wanted; we wanted to see this foreigner flattened, put in his place. And then everything could go back to normal: the new kid would be new no longer; we could all leave him alone and start thinking about something else. Maybe our Phony War, as we were calling it, would become a real one.

"Come on, then," said Stinky. He was almost yawning with boredom.

"Go ahead and hit me first," said Bleeker.

"Daft sod," Charlie whispered to me. "If Stinky plows him one, then the fight's over."

"No, you," said Stinky. "Gimme your best shot." Stinky liked American gangster movies, too, the same as the rest of us.

The crowd started yelling. "Get Mr. Big, Stinky!"

"Annihilate him!"

"Kill him!"

They pushed the two combatants from behind, trying to get them started. Bleeker fell into Stinky's unwilling fists. Stinky gave him a cuff on the cheek with the palm of his hand, which did no damage but must have stung. You could say what you like about Corcoran, but he wasn't a dirty fighter. He was big and he was fast, and he could punish anyone who got him mad, but I'd never seen him fight dirty; he didn't need to.

Dirty fighting meant punching below the belt, or using your elbows, knees, or feet—kicking was the worst thing you could possibly do. First-class cowards ran away; second-class cowards kicked. Clean fighting was fists only, like James Cagney in *City for Conquest* or like William Holden in *Golden Boy*.

Bleeker brushed away the slap, pretending it was nothing, pushed his dirty black hair out of his eyes, and stepped back, fists up, protecting his chin.

Stinky must have decided to get it over with as quickly as possible, because he stepped in fast and thumped Bleeker hard in the belly, not low under the belt—as I said, Stinky didn't fight dirty—but higher, in the breadbasket, taking all the wind out of Bleeker, and causing him to double over, gasping with pain.

The crowd went, "Whooo!"

That one blow should have been the end of it. It was fast and it was hard. It would be no disgrace for Bleeker if he were to stay down. The crowd, watching Bleeker in

8

pain, was now less bloodthirsty. We all knew it was a mis-match, and perhaps we felt a bit guilty. So none of us would have minded too much if Bleeker had just sat down on the grass nursing his pain, fighting for his breath, crying perhaps—we would've liked that—while Stinky grabbed his jacket off the top of the monkey bars and went home.

"Fight's over!" shouted Two-Ply.

But it wasn't over. That one blow wasn't to be the end of it.

Bleeker surprised us all by rushing at Stinky like an angry Spitfire spotting a Heinkel. All eight guns firing, he took Stinky by surprise. Stinky didn't know what hit him. What hit him was Bleeker's fist, flattening his nose and drawing a quick gush of blood.

"Aaaaaahhhhh!" cried Stinky. He clapped both hands to his face. The old red stuff flowed through his fingers. He looked at his bloody hands in astonishment. No one had ever hit him and drawn blood before.

We all held our breath while Stinky stared at his bloody hands. We saw him get madder and madder. Ignoring the blood flowing from his nose, he became a one-man blitzkrieg, charging at Bleeker, fists whirling.

"Go easy!" someone yelled.

"Give the man a chance, why don't yer!"

"Give it to him, Stinky!"

"Throw in the towel, Bleeker!" shouted Two-Ply.

Bleeker didn't stand a chance against Stinky's anger or his demon speed and weight. Bleeker was fast, but not fast enough to avoid two hard thumps to the head, one on each side, from Stinky's big fists. He reeled and almost fell. Stinky hit him again, one-two! Fists as big as a grown man's. This time Bleeker fell to his knees, but immediately staggered up again as though the ground was the red-hot sizzling hob of hell.

"Stay down, Bleeker!" someone shouted.

There was blood on the side of his face, on the same side as his black eye, which had started closing up again. Unsteady on his feet, swaying, he put up his fists and faced Stinky.

"Crazy bugger!" yelled Gordie beside me.

Stinky was holding his head back to stop the flow of blood from his nose and wiping the blood off his face with his sleeves, which he had rolled down. He wasn't expecting any further trouble from his opponent. When he saw Bleeker standing with his fists up, ready for more, he looked puzzled. He advanced. Bleeker struck out at him feebly with his right hand, missed, and followed it with a left, which also missed. Bleeker backed away, stumbling, playing for time, trying to gather strength.

"Give up, Mr. Big!" someone shouted. "Stinky'll murder yer!"

Stinky came after him, bomb doors fully open. Bleeker managed to get in under the blows and fire a rapid one-two-three at Stinky's ribs. Stinky pushed him off and feinted with his left. Bleeker saw the right coming and tried to recover, but it was too late: Stinky had set him up for a fast uppercut that took Bleeker under the jaw and rattled his teeth.

Again Bleeker went down, on one knee. I could see

fresh blood on his lip where it had been punctured by a tooth.

We waited, watching for Stinky to declare the fight over by turning his back on the bleeding Bleeker and grabbing his coat, but Bleeker was up! Wobbly, eyes glazed, raising his fists by an effort of will, he faced Stinky.

Stinky glared at him. Bleeker spat blood out of his mouth and advanced on Stinky, fists like new potatoes. Stinky hit him a hard roundhouse right to the side of the head.

Bleeker was stopped in his tracks. Then, to make certain, Stinky walloped him with a wicked left hook that caught him under the ear. Bleeker whirled with the force of the blow, staggered, and went down onto his back.

Silence.

We waited. That had to be it.

Bleeker rolled over, and climbed painfully onto his knees. Then, after a pause, he pushed himself upright and stood unsteadily on his feet with his back to Stinky. Realizing he was facing in the wrong direction, he turned, almost falling, and faced his tormentor.

This time it was an even greater effort, but his trembling fists went up, signaling his opponent that the fight was not yet over.

We couldn't believe it. Everyone stopped breathing.

Usually, in a fight like this, with a fighter who refused to give in, we would all be yelling and shouting to beat the band. But not today. You could've heard a grasshopper scratch his arse: we were guilty and silent. Bleeker was out on his feet; he was dead, but he wouldn't lie down.

11

Everyone could see that Stinky didn't want to fight anymore. The bleeding from his nose had stopped, but he stood there with his bloody fists unclenched, looking at Bleeker as though the Irish kid was crazy. He turned to the crowd, puzzled, not sure what to do next.

Charlie McCauley stepped in. He grabbed the wrists of both fighters and held them aloft. "I declare this fight a draw," he said formally, like a referee.

Stinky looked puzzled.

We yelled and cheered.

Stinky grinned.

The crowd converged on the fighters, slapping their backs, pumping their hands. "Well done, Bleeker!" We weren't calling him Mr. Big anymore. "Well done, Stinky!"

And then—you'd think the Holy Ghost and all the saints had been watching us!—the air-raid siren started its high-pitched moan.

The crowd broke up. Some of the smaller kids ran off in a hurry, their gas masks bumping on their behinds.

"It'll be another false alarm," said Gordie.

Too big to be seen carrying gas masks, we'd stopped months ago when it was obvious we wouldn't be needing them.

I handed Bleeker his scruffy jacket. He took it without looking at me. We walked together, me, Bleeker, Charlie, Bren, and Gordie, out of the playground and down the alley—the back jigger we called it—that led into Leinster Road.

"Good fight, Bleeker," said Gordie as he left us, taking

off in the direction of Broadgreen Road. "See youse to-morrow."

When we came out the back jigger to where the rest of us all lived, Baden Road, Charlie said, "See youse later, Jamie?"

I nodded and answered for both myself and Bren. "Later. We'll come over."

Bren and I turned, intending to walk the rest of the way with Bleeker, but he'd hurried on ahead, not waiting for us. I could see his straight back in its man's jacket moving away down the street.

"Good fight, Bleeker," Charlie shouted after him.

But he didn't turn.

We stood and watched him disappear into number 17.

TWO

It had been another false alarm right enough. Old Mr. Murphy, who lived in number 15, was standing out in the street, hand shading his eyes against the sun. I looked up. All I could see was a lone Lysander humming and throbbing in the high air above the silver-gray barrage balloons. No Jerries. Mr. Murphy saw me and Bren and said the air-raid wardens must have mistaken the Lysander for a German Stuka or a Heinkel. He laughed. "They must be pissed."

"Tarrah well," I said to Bren as he made for his back door. "Tarrah well" means "goodbye" in Scouse, which is what they speak in Liverpool. A Liverpool person is called a Scouser, don't ask me why.

The all-clear signal started warbling as I got in the house. Mrs. Costello from Crofton Crescent was sitting in the cane chair in the kitchen, her loaded shopping bag at her feet. My mam was making her a cup of tea.

"You're just in time for a cup, Jamie," said my mam. "Go up and change first."

Mrs. Costello leaned forward and peered at my legs.

"It's in the long trouser you are, Jamie." She looked up at my mam. "Ah, they grow up terrible fast, they do, isn't it the truth."

I looked down at my gray trousers. I'd been in longs for over a year. I wasn't a kid anymore. Mrs. Costello was a forgetful old lady, one of my mam's older, gray-haired pensioner pals—old biddies my dad called them—who once or twice a week pushed open our yard door and shouted, "Are you in, Mrs. Monaghan?," my mam responding with an "I'm just putting on the kettle, Mrs. Costello, come on in."

I hung my cap and blazer on the peg in the hall, went up and took off the rest of my school uniform—black leather shoes, white shirt, tie, trousers—and pulled on a jersey, old navy blue trousers, and sneakers.

A cup of tea and a couple of jam butties were waiting when I got downstairs. I carried them into the kitchen and started on my homework, which was only algebra. Most of the kids never bothered to do algebra homework because it was hardly ever checked. Miss O'Hara just read out the answers while the kids pretended to mark them. Occasionally, however, she did check, which is why I always did the work; best to play it safe.

It was hard to concentrate with Mrs. Costello's foghorn voice.

". . . three killed in one week according to the *Echo*, knocked down in the blackout, didn't know what hit 'em, I shouldn't wonder, so the poor woman is lucky to be alive at all."

"Where is she?" My mam.

"Whipped her into Broadgreen Hospital they did, in the ambylance, broken hip and I don't know what else, with all the bandages you wouldn't know her, there's more killed by cars in the blackout than by Hitler's bombs, I swear to God . . ."

I gathered my book and papers together and went back upstairs.

By the time I had the homework finished, Mrs. Costello had gone and my mam was busy starting the dinner.

I got Bren from next door and we went over to Charlie's house. We kicked a ball around for a bit until Gordie arrived, with his stick as usual. He didn't take it to school with him, but Gordie had a stick as tall as himself with one end sharpened and a rubber grip halfway down that he'd taken off the handlebars of an old bike; it was his spear, in case a German paratrooper fell out of the sky. We'd all told him months ago he was wasting his time, that there'd be no Germans, but the stick had become a part of him.

"Come on," said Charlie, "let's sneak into the side door of the Regent."

But the cinema usher was on guard and we had to run for it, ending up in Gordie's backyard air-raid shelter which Gordie's dad had fixed up, cozy almost, like a den, with a table and chairs, and carpet remnants from Lewis's on the concrete floor.

We talked for a long time about Bleeker and the fight, and the way Charlie had declared it a draw, and the puzzled look on Stinky's face. "That was quick thinking, Charlie," said Gordie, "rushing in like that and making it like a real professional match." His stick stood in the corner, ready should he need it.

Gordie's sister, Gloria, tip-tapped down the yard on her high heels. Charlie was the first out the shelter and into the yard; me and Bren weren't far behind. "Hi, Gloria," said Charlie. "Your stockings are crooked."

Gloria stopped and looked at us. She smiled at Charlie. She was all dressed up, didn't even bother to look over her shoulder to check her seams: she knew they were straight.

Gloria was nineteen, a real gorgeous bit of all right with long dark hair and big blue eyes, built long and slim, like a Wellington bomber with two power-operated gun turrets.

We talked about girls a lot. Girls were a mystery, like the Blessed Trinity, only more interesting. They were one of our main topics of conversation, me and Charlie and Bren straining eagerly to learn from Gordie what it was like to live with such a smashing piece of stuff day in and day out; it must be a real education, we said, a sight for sore eyes, having a front-row seat, so to speak, to all Gloria's comings and goings and all her—do you ever see her—you know—in the—you know—undressed? What was it like? Gordie never said much, but admitted reluctantly that, yes, he did get to see a lot of stuff, but would never say what, only making a gesture or two with his

17

hands that drove us wild in our ignorance. We never had quite the same interest in Bren's two older sisters, who were just nice, ordinary girls lacking Gloria's mystery and glamour.

"I've got a date," said Gloria to Charlie. "Want to come?" She laughed.

"Who with? Dave Gibson, I bet," said Charlie. Dave was in the RAF, stationed at an air force base somewhere down south; he wasn't allowed to say where, we all knew that, and Gloria had been going out with him ever since he'd signed on a year ago to do battle with the Hun. He wasn't even a Spitfire pilot; he was an ACHGD, Aircraft Hand General Duties, which Gloria said was an important job with airplanes, but which Charlie's dad, who had been in the air force, said was what they called the twerps who cleaned out the bogs, which is what we called the shithouse when adults were around.

Gloria smiled. "He wangled a forty-eight-hour pass. We're going dancing at the Rialto." She glanced at her wristwatch, then waved four fingers at us, and turned to go. "Tarrah well."

"Tarrah well." We watched her go.

The backyard gate rattled on its latch as it closed behind her.

"Phew!" said Charlie.

"Phew!" echoed me and Bren.

Gordie, his stick in his hand, just stood there like King Neptune with his trident.

· · ·

When I got home, my dad was there, fiddling with the wireless, trying to rescue Lord Haw-Haw's voice from the static. I don't know if he was called Haw-Haw because of the way he spoke—like a braying ass with a phony posh accent—or because people in England laughed, haw-haw, at his attempts to scare them. His real name was William Joyce, and he was a British traitor.

"I don't know why you have to listen to that jackeen every night," said my mam. "It's nothing but muck. Jamie, set the table for dinner, please."

My dad said nothing, his ear to the receiver.

I could hear Lord Haw-Haw's voice coming through from Germany a little more clearly but couldn't make out what he was saying even though I wasn't rattling the knives and forks.

The static cleared for a moment and I could hear the end of the broadcast.

". . . lay down your arms!" said Lord Haw-Haw. "Resistance is useless! The people of England will curse themselves for having preferred ruin from Churchill to peace from Hitler!"

There was more, but I didn't catch it. My dad switched off the wireless. He was frowning.

"You don't believe that stuff, do you, Dad?" I said. "Nobody else does. They laugh at him."

My mam came in from the kitchen and stood by me. We watched my dad.

"London is on fire," said my dad.

"What?" said my mam.

"The whole city's on fire, amn't I telling you?"

"Ha!" said my mam. "Don't tell me you're starting to believe Lord Haw-Haw! He's nothing but a jackeen and a liar."

"Listen to me, woman! It's not talking about Haw-Haw I am. I heard it from a feller on a ship up today from Southampton. The whole city of London is on fire!"

I watched the small slanting line on his forehead that told me he was really worried.

"They don't tell us everything on the news, Nan, you know that. Wave after wave of bombers, hundreds and hundreds of them, bombing the bejaysus out of them, that's what he said."

"Jack! That's no kind of language in front of a child!"

"The East End of London is destroyed, woman. There's thousands killed. And as many homeless, wandering the streets. People are leaving their homes every day before the bombing starts, grabbing their kids and their blankets, and they're all off traipsing to the countryside, pushing prams, riding on buses, hitching, anything to get away."

"Countryside?" My mam seemed to be in a state of shock.

"Where it's safe," said my dad.

"But where do they sleep?" said my mam.

"Anywhere, woman. In ditches, in barns, wherever they can. It doesn't matter where they sleep so long as they're safe from the bombs."

There was a silence. My mam dried her dry hands with the tea cloth.

"In the morning when the raid is over, they go back home." My dad rubbed at his brow. "Until the evening, and then off they go again."

"They won't bomb Liverpool again," said my mam. "It's a terrible long way for them to come." She stared with round-eyed uncertainty at my dad. "Isn't it, Jack?"

THREE

The next day at school, Bleeker was more popular than Winston Churchill. He was one of us now. No more Mr. Big. He was plain Bleeker. He was accepted. Not that it changed him—it didn't: he was still the same old Bleeker, tough and scowling, and seemed to take everyone's admiration as his due.

Beryl Oyler, the most beautiful girl in the class, and indeed the whole school, sat next to him during drawing—the only time Miss O'Hara let us move our desks and sit wherever we liked so we could draw the still life from our own chosen angle. I sat behind them, not to eavesdrop, of course, but because Bleeker was interesting. Beryl was interesting, too.

Today we were drawing a big vase with four spiky crimson dahlias in it. The vase sat atop a high stool. Around the base of the vase were scattered oak leaves brought in by Miss O'Hara from the school yard.

"I'm going to be a nurse," Beryl whispered to Bleeker. They were very close.

Bleeker didn't answer her. He was concentrating on his drawing. I peeked over his shoulder. He wasn't drawing the flowers but was trying to copy the Spitfire from the poster on the wall behind.

"I will bathe and cleanse the wounds of our brave soldiers," said Beryl in a phrase she had probably picked up from one of those soppy stories in the *Girls' Own Annual*.

"Mhhn," said Bleeker.

Beryl stopped drawing to gaze at Bleeker's bruises with a sympathetic and professional eye. She wore a blue wool sweater, soft and scented. I could sit and inhale it all day and not draw a line. I watched her profile: milky cheek, full pink lips, black curling eyelashes, brown eyes brimming with compassion. I sighed, almost wishing it had been me—I—who had fought Stinky Corcoran. I watched her dimpled white hand with its plump little wrist flutter for a second in the air near Bleeker's bruised cheek as though about to alight there, but then she turned back to her drawing and returned the hand to its perch on the edge of the desk.

Bleeker had noticed nothing or, if he had, wasn't letting on.

Out in the yard at lunchtime, lots of kids talked to Bleeker, but he answered them curtly and they let him alone. Charlie and I went up to him. Charlie said, "I gotta hand it to you, Bleeker, you're the toughest fighter I ever saw, standing up to Corcoran the way you did. You

23

were great. Reminded me of James Cagney in—what was that boxing movie, Jamie?"

"Mhhn," said Bleeker. "You're the galoot who stopped the fight."

"Huh?" Charlie didn't like the "galoot" bit.

"Maybe you oughtta mind your own business in future," Bleeker growled.

Charlie's face fell. "What do you mean?"

Bleeker pushed his ugly face into Charlie's. "I mean you had no business stopping the fight. I don't need no help from anyone. I could've beat him if you hadn't interfered." He gave Charlie a push in the chest that sent him staggering back. Then he shot me a withering look, turned on his heel, and swaggered off.

"Not a friendly person," I said to Charlie.

"I'm glad it's you lives next door to him and not me."

In the afternoon, Bleeker and Stinky Corcoran were sent for: Mr. Hale, the headmaster, wanted them down in his office.

We all looked at each other; we knew what it meant: Mr. Hale must have heard about the fight. Excited whispers hissed around the class. What would happen? Did it mean the strap? Mr. Hale's strap was feared more than Hitler's gas. It was made of a heavy black leather, dark brown at the edges and shiny with use, shaped and curved, with a handle, and it looked to be very old. I had only ever had it once, one on each hand, for sagging—skipping—school one afternoon, and that was enough: I never wanted to have it again. No, Bleeker and Stinky wouldn't be strapped, some thought, because the fight

24

wasn't in the school yard. What then? A stern lecture? Wait and see if they returned to class with white faces and purple palms.

They were gone a long time. "A lecture," whispered Bren.

"A lecture *and* the strap!" said Two-Ply.

Bleeker was first through the door. Nonchalantly he swaggered back to his desk and sat down. Corcoran loped in like a grizzly bear, arms hanging, and wedged himself back into his desk with a grunt.

We could all see that they hadn't been strapped, so immediately lost interest.

At four o'clock Mr. Hale stepped out of his office into the hallway and rang the bell the way he always did at the end of the day. It was a handbell made of heavy brass, and it didn't ring or rattle or clang the way most bells do; it boomed along the hallways and up the stairs to the second floor of the school, where I was in Miss O'Hara's class.

Classroom doors flew open and hundreds of feet pounded down the wooden stairs, out the door, down Snozzy's worn granite steps, and into the warm, waiting sunshine.

I waited with Charlie until Bren and Gordie caught up, and then we turned for the playground and home.

Bleeker walked a little way ahead with his sister.

"Let's catch up and ask him what happened in Hale's office," Bren suggested.

"I don't think so," said Charlie, still cheesed off because Bleeker had called him a galoot.

25

But Bren had already yelled, "Wait up, Bleeker!"

He stopped, looked back, and waited for us to catch up.

"So how did you like Mr. Hale's boring old lecture?" said Bren. "What did he say—'Good Catholics don't fight'?"

"Or was it 'A Catholic boy should set an example'?" said Gordie.

The little sister was whining, and pulling at Bleeker to keep walking.

Bleeker ignored her. He scowled at me and Charlie, shot Gordie a suspicious look, and then turned to Bren. "Mr. Hale is right. People shouldn't fight. If people didn't fight, there wouldn't be no war."

"What!" said Charlie. "And let Hitler walk all over us! Are you crazy?"

Bleeker said, "Are you calling me crazy?"

"No, but—"

"You better watch it, galoot. Anyway, Hitler's a people. If he didn't fight, then we wouldn't fight, would we? We gotta fight him back because it was him who started it." He scowled at Charlie, challenging him to argue.

"Hitler's not people," said Charlie, "Hitler's a monster, everyone knows that."

This time it was me who stepped in. "Come on, let's see who can swing a miss-two-bars-there-and-back on the monkey bars," and I pushed on hoping they'd all follow.

They did. When we got to the playground, Bren said, "You coming in with us, Bleeker?"

He shook his head. "Gotta get home."

Charlie and Bren and Gordie ran into the playground, but I stood for a few seconds at the gate watching Bleeker walk off. He didn't know I was watching. Elsie's hand in his, he dropped the swagger, hunched his shoulders, and headed slowly down the back jigger toward Baden Road.

The air-raid siren howled.

"Get up, Jamie!" yelled my mam. "Quick, will ye!" She left the burning candle by the clock and hurried downstairs.

I squinted at the alarm clock. Midnight. It had to be another false alarm: the sirens never went this late.

Half-asleep, I rolled from my warm bed, struggled into pants and jersey, and traipsed down the stairs, yawning, the candle holder with its burning candle in my hand.

The house was cold. My mam was making tea in the kitchen. She hadn't lit the gaslight because of the blackout but had a candle burning on the top of the copper washboiler. I set my candle down beside hers. My dad was sitting on the back step with Bren's dad, Mr. O'Dougherty, from next door. They were smoking their Woodbines and looking up at the sky. Cigs were scarce. Mr. Fell, the tobacconist, hid them under the counter for his regulars. My dad worked on the docks, though, and dockers were never short; he sold a few to Mr. O'Dougherty whenever he had any extra.

I stood in the kitchen, still half-asleep, shoulders hunched against the cold, watching my mam make the tea.

"False alarm," I said.

"Don't be so sure," said my mam. "Fetch a shovelful of coal and light the fire. Make yourself useful."

I pushed my way through the two men on the back step and fetched the coal and a bit of kindling from the coal bin at the bottom of the yard.

The sirens were still wailing.

I tore up an old *Liverpool Echo,* set the fire in the grate, and stood on the fender watching the wood catch alight. It crackled and sparked, but over the noise of the fire and the screams of the sirens I could hear something else, a whine or a drone more like, getting louder as I stood staring into the flames.

It was planes. Bombers! Sounded like a thousand of them pounding up the river.

A real air raid!

I couldn't believe it. Did this mean the Phony War was over? That the real war was about to start? Brilliant! Smashing!

Bursts of gunfire from the Springfield Park ground artillery, *ack-ack-ack.* What a row! I was fully awake now.

"Can I come out?" I yelled to my dad.

"No."

"Just for a quick look."

"No! Get to bed under the stair."

"I'll bring ye a cup of tea," whispered my mam, wide-eyed, scared.

The blackout curtains were up. I poked my head out the door. Dad didn't see me in the dark. I looked up. You wouldn't think there was a blackout: the sky glowed a sizzling green with parachute flares dropped by the

28

bombers. I could see the Big Nellies—barrage balloons—drifting on the ends of their cables, caught in the searchlight beams as they swept the unclouded sky for planes.

I saw one. A bomber. The searchlight had him good. Too far away to see the German cross on the fuselage, but it was a Jerry all right. The anti-aircraft guns pounded away at him. Bursts of flak underneath.

"Junkers 88!" I said.

And then he was gone, slipping the searchlight beam like a dog off its leash.

"They lost him!" said my dad in disgust.

"Sly divils," said Mr. O'Dougherty.

We stared at the sky, alive with green and orange lights, white searchlight beams, gleaming balloons, puffs of smoke.

"Sure it's grand, Jack!" said Mr. O'Dougherty to my dad, rubbing his hands together excitedly.

"Better than the Blackpool fireworks," said my dad.

"It's smashin'," I agreed.

I didn't know if it had really been a Junkers. Too dark, and too far away. Could have been a Dornier or a Heinkel for all I knew, but I was hoping my dad would find use for an expert and allow me to stay outside; he knew I studied aircraft ID charts all the time.

My mam gave us all mugs of tea.

I could hear a woman yelling.

Mam tapped Dad on the shoulder. "See what she wants, will ye, Jack. It's the new woman at the Sharps'."

The Sharps used to live next door in number 17, but

they moved away three weeks ago. Went back to Ireland. There had been only the two of them. Mrs. Sharp had been preggo. With child. Balloon over the toyshop, as my Uncle Larry used to say. After the Sharps left, the Bleekers moved in almost right away. My mam, not one to push her nose in, hadn't spoken yet to the new neighbors because the woman hardly ever came out of the house. And when she did come out with her shopping bag over her arm, she was gone off down the road like a Hawker Hurricane before anyone could stop her to say hello.

"What's the young boy like?" my mam had asked me soon after they'd moved in.

I shrugged.

"How old is he?"

"Same as me."

"What about the wee one?"

I shrugged again.

"Did ye see the dad yet?"

"No."

"Sure I'll meet them soon enough," said my mam.

Now, with the air raid going on, my dad was standing on tiptoes and peering over the next-door wall. "What is it, missus?" he shouted. "Are ye all right?"

The woman said something I couldn't hear because of all the noise going on. Then Dad said something, stepped back from the wall, and walked down the yard to open the back gate.

The new woman came into our yard. She was preggo. Must be something to do with that house, number 17. Balloon for a belly. The two kids with her. She had the little one by the hand, and in her other hand she carried their gas masks. Bleeker's face was even more of a toilet bowl than usual because of the swollen lip and all the new bruises. He glared at me.

They followed my dad up the yard, the sky behind them now red and orange from fires. Incendiary bombs.

I knew about incendiaries from the Movietone news at the Regent Cinema. Small, about a foot long, thirty-six of them to a bomb casing, they showered down and came through your roof. Next thing your house was ablaze.

". . . air-raid shelter," Dad was saying to Mam. He nodded at our supposedly bombproof brick shelter.

I caught on. The Bleekers wanted to use our shelter. There was none next door because the Sharps had told the Civil Defence they didn't want one, that they'd use their stairs.

"Ye're welcome to it," said my mam to Mrs. Bleeker, "though it's terrible damp. Throw the bikes out, Jack, and I'll put in a few chairs." To me she said, "Bring the gas masks."

Dad started to move stuff out of the shelter. I went to check on the fire, fetch our masks from the cupboard in the kitchen, and help my mam with the chairs, carrying them out to the shelter. Our backyard was tiny, with no soil or garden, just tiles. Which was why we couldn't have an Anderson shelter; for an Anderson you needed to dig out a deep trench, and bolt the corrugated, curved steel sheets together, then pile a couple of feet of earth over the top. People said that the Andersons were safer. Brick shelters like ours took up half the yard. They were ugly, too, with a concrete roof a foot thick. We used ours for storage.

Dad had taken the bikes out of our shelter and propped them up against the wall that divided us from number 17 next door—his, the BSA he went to work on, and mine, a rusty old Raleigh with no mudguards. Then he pulled out some old lumber and other rubbish, and the woman went in with her kids. There was no light in the shelter. They sat on the chairs in the dark.

"Thanks very much," said Mrs. Bleeker.

"Ye're more than welcome," said my mam to the woman's shape in the darkness.

Funny. It was like they were in a posh drawing room like you'd see in a movie, except the lights had gone out, all polite, their voices raised a bit because of the noise, but otherwise so calm you'd never think there was holy murder going on over our heads.

"Wait and I'll get ye a bit of candle," said my mam.

"Please don't—"

"Sure, it's no trouble."

She was back in a jiff with a lighted candle, cushions, and blankets.

"We never use the shelter," Mam explained. "Too cold and damp. We sit under the stair."

"Under the stair?" said Mrs. Bleeker, puzzled. The little girl was sitting on her mam's knees, clutching a doll and whining that she was cold. "Thank you," said Mrs. Bleeker, taking a blanket and wrapping it about the girl.

Mam said, "When the Jerries started bombing London, the Civil Defence workers found whole families alive under the stair, and the houses collapsed on top of them, nothing but bricks and rubble. It was in the paper, so it was. I'm Nan Monaghan, and this is my husband, Jack. Matt O'Dougherty's from number 21." She jerked her head toward the house next door. "And this is Jamie," she finished, laying a hand on my shoulder.

"Mary Bleeker," said the woman. Her eye, I noticed now, was bruised yellow-violet, a shiner, almost healed. "Brian's out tonight," she said. "Won't be back till late." She held her head so the purpled eye was away from the candlelight. "This is Elsie." She stroked the girl's head. "And Tom." She nodded at Bleeker. "He's been fighting at school."

I could see Bleeker better in the candlelight—yellow, like one of them—those—pictures by the Dutch painter, Remnant, or some name like that. His face was a mess. His lower lip where the tooth had gone through was puffed and purple, and the eye that had been blacked was now blacker, closed and shining like a flashlight. With his one good eye he saw me looking at the bruises, and glared at me. Tough. I had to admit it: he scared me.

Mam looked at me sharpish. "Fighting? Do ye know anything about this, Jamie?"

I opened my eyes real wide, innocent. "Who, me?"

I suddenly figured out where Bleeker and his mam got their shiners from: it was the noise and the fights that went on at night. The wall between the houses was thin. We'd heard them arguing and fighting several times in the two weeks they'd been there. Shouts and screams. Furniture thrown about. "The new feller's a drunk," Dad had said. "Is there nothing we can do?" said Mam. "Go out and fetch a policeman maybe," Dad said. But we knew the fight would be long over by the time we could find one, so we did nothing. Besides, it was an unwritten rule among the Irish in Liverpool: you didn't tell tales on your own. Kind of like James Cagney in an American gangster movie, covering for Humphrey Bogart, not ratting to the villain, Edward G. Robinson.

"I'm cold," whined Elsie. The doll clutched in her arms was an old homemade rag of a thing, long and loose-jointed.

Bleeker gave little pulls on the doll's floppy legs, pretending it wasn't him, but Elsie didn't want to play; she whined, and jerked the doll away from her brother's teasing fingers.

The night wasn't cold, but the dampness of the shelter was chilling.

"I'll bring ye some tea," said my mam now, pretending not to notice Mrs. Bleeker's bruised face, "and one of Jamie's jerseys for the wee one."

"Ah, don't trouble yourself," said Mrs. Bleeker.

"The shelter's cold, so it is," said Mam. "It's no trouble."

I looked at Bleeker. He had stopped teasing his sister and was picking his nose.

Mam went in the house.

"Stop that!" said Mrs. Bleeker, slapping her son's hand away from his nose.

34

Bleeker gave a sniff, and glared at me like it was me who'd slapped him.

The bombs started. I heard a whistling sound, and saw a flash over toward the docks and the shipyards, and another over by the gasworks.

A real raid at last! I felt the excitement fizzing in me.

Mr. O'Dougherty said, "I'm off!" He dashed away down the yard and out the gate, back to his own house and family.

Dad had forgotten I was there. He saw me and got that wild look in his eyes, the one he gets just before he wallops me one. "Amn't I just after telling ye—!" I jumped back into the house and under the stairs, and climbed into the bunk my dad rigged up a few months ago for me, right after Lord Haw-Haw first said on the wireless that the Luftwaffe, the German air force, was going to destroy England.

My mam took a jersey and some tea out to the Bleekers, and then she and my dad came into the house and sat on the floor under my bunk. My mam had her Jacob's tin biscuit box with all her important papers in it. "We maybe should sit in the shelter with the Bleekers," said my mam to my dad. "Keep them company."

"They'll be fine," said my dad.

My blood was wild. I wanted to be outside: I wanted to see everything. I wanted to see a German plane belching fire as it dropped down a searchlight beam like a number two spinning down the toilet. I wanted to see incendiaries raining down, I wanted . . .

Because of the blackout my dad hadn't turned on the

gaslight in the living room, but the fire I'd lit was going strong, and the firelight flickering into the hall lit my mam's face. She still looked scared. She was sitting with her back to the hallway, facing my dad. I couldn't see his face so well because of the shadows. I saw him reach over and loop his arm around her.

A whistle! Louder this time. The whistle stopped.

Silence.

I could feel my heart hammering.

A shuddering roar. Crunch! The house shook. I heard glass breaking.

"Jesus, Mary, and Joseph!" said my mam.

"That wasn't far away!" said my dad, his voice tight.

Then another. The noise made my ears ring. The house shook again. Glass breaking in a shattering explosion. I covered my ears with my hands, and lay in my bunk, knees drawn up to my chest.

Whistle! Crump!

A sound like a sheet ripped in half. Then a hail of shrapnel or debris striking the roof.

Another. Not so loud. Farther away this time. The house trembled. Something crashed in the living room.

"Chamberlain!" said my mam. "I forgot all about him!" She started to get up, but my dad pulled her back down. "Stay where ye are, Nan. The cat can look after itself."

Chamberlain slunk into the hallway and crept under the stairs, crying at my mam. She pulled him onto her lap. He lay there, eyes wide and staring, tail twitching. Big ugly tabby tomcat. Too old for war. I reached down and felt his velvet ears between thumb and forefinger.

Smell of burnt sausages. Smell of soot.

There was soot in the hall. I choked.

"They've cleaned the chimney for us," said my dad, coughing.

My mam groaned. "The soot'll be into everything."

I could hear more bombs dropping farther away. Then nothing. Everything went quiet.

"They missed us," said my dad. He was being funny. He still had his arm around my mam.

We waited in the silence.

Dad got up and went into the living room. "We're destroyed with the soot, Nan," he called.

"Jack!" Mam shouted. "Come back under the stair, will ye."

"I will," said my dad. His voice came from the back step. He was outside looking at the sky again.

"Can I go see?" I said to my mam.

"Stay where ye are. The all-clear hasn't gone; the planes might be back." She got up and went out to the kitchen. I could hear her. "Jack, come in! Ye're worse than a child!"

I slipped out of my bunk and went the opposite way, through the hallway and the vestibule to the front door, past the gas meter that my mam kept fed at the rate of a bob a day. A bob was a shilling. I eased the door open, not wanting the wee brass lion knocker to give me away, and stepped out onto the street.

The sky was bright, red like blood. It looked like the whole city was on fire.

My mam was right. They were coming back. I could

hear them, a thundering pulse. I dashed back inside and scrambled into my bunk in the dark not a second too soon, for my mam and dad followed almost right after.

The Jerries must have turned. I tried to imagine hundreds of planes turning at night, turning for home, back to Germany, or was it France? Paris fell in June. I remember because it was near the end of the school year, before the holidays. The Luftwaffe had airfields now in France, right across the English Channel. Did the turning planes still have bombs they hadn't dropped?

They did.

The noise started up again: the drum of the planes, the pounding of the guns, the bombs whistling down and exploding and rocking the street with their blast.

How could I have thought it was a whistle they made as they fell? More like a scream. We were surrounded by screams, high-pitched, heart-stopping screams, buried under the terrible din of them.

"God save us!" my mam muttered.

"It's the docks the stupid jackeens are supposed to be destroying, not the library," said my dad.

The house shuddered. More breaking glass. Plaster and dust from the hallway ceiling. The rattle of shrapnel and debris on the roof.

"Are ye all right, Jamie?" said my mam. She was scared, I could hear it in her voice. I wanted to tell her it was all right, nothing to be scared about, only a raid, hadn't we been waiting for them to come for over a year?

I started mumbling Hail Mary's to myself as fast as I could, one after the other. For my mam, I told myself.

And my dad. Which was strange, for I'd never been one for praying. At school when the prayers were said, me and Bren and Charlie and Gordie always recited "The boy stood on the burning deck, his underpants on fire," and old Annie Tracy, the teacher we had last year, never knew we weren't saying our prayers like the rest of them.

We waited for the rumble of the planes to pass and for the house to stop shaking. Mam looked like she was praying, too.

The noise eventually stopped. The planes had gone.

"They'll not be back," said my dad.

We waited.

Dad went out to the back again. I heard him talking to someone. The new people, the Bleekers, in the shelter.

It was dark. The soot had doused the fire.

The siren sounded the all-clear.

I could hear voices in the street. And the whistles of the ARP wardens, who were old geezers and old biddies responsible for the supervision of air-raid precautions, the ones who hammered on your door if light was escaping through your blackout curtains.

"Thank God it's over," said my mam. "I'll make a cup of tea."

I moved my legs. Something damp.

I'd peed the bed.

FOUR

I wanted to go outside and see the damage, but my dad said no.

"It's still dangerous out there," said my mam.

The Bleekers had gone back to their own house.

"How can it be dangerous?" I argued. "The raid is over. I bet all me friends—"

My dad's eyes grew round. He didn't like me talking back. And he didn't like me talking like a Scouser. " '*Me* friends' is it! It's the real Liverpool bucko ye're turning into! 'Me leg, me knee, me elbow'! It's *my* belt I'll be wrapping round *your* backside if ye don't watch your tongue!"

At school and with my friends I did my best to sound Scouse—I wanted to be the same as them—but sometimes I forgot and spoke Scouse at home. My mam didn't like it either; she thought it sounded common.

Matt O'Dougherty came in, poking his black head

around the door. "God save all here," he said in the traditional Irish house greeting.

He had his kids with him, Brensley, Pat, and Madeleine, except Madeleine wasn't a kid, she was old, way over twenty. She was very friendly with my mam.

"Are ye all right, Nan?" Madeleine said, looking around at all the soot and plaster and broken glass. "I'll put on the kettle." Which was what she always said whenever she popped in, once or twice a day.

I liked Madeleine. She had long, thick red hair, usually worn in a single plait down her back, and she was big, with a ruddy, cheerful face.

My mam and dad liked to hear her sing, which she often did, sitting at the kitchen table with a cup of tea in front of her. She'd sing "Kathleen Mavourneen," or "The Rose of Tralee," or some old Irish rebel thing like "Kelly, the Boy from Kilane," a marching song, and one of her favorites. I don't know who Kelly was, but according to the song he was a hero. Madeleine pronounced it Kil*ann*. "Tell me who's the giant with the gold curling hair," she sang, "he who rides at the head of the van. Seven feet is his height with some inches to spare, and he looks like a king in command."

Madeleine with her fiery red curling hair and flashing eyes.

The Irish seemed to have a lot of freedom songs.

When Madeleine finished singing, Dad would smile and say, "Ah, that was powerful, Madeleine, so it was. It's the gift ye have and no mistake." And Mam would shake her head as though she couldn't believe anyone who

41

wasn't sent straight down from heaven by the Archangel Gabriel himself could sing so well. "It was, sure it was just lovely."

Madeleine's sister, Pat, had brown hair and a pale face. She was a year older than me. Brensley, the youngest, same age as me, had a big high quiff of black hair that always fell over one eye in spite of all the Brylcreem he slathered on it. We'd been friends, me and Bren, since we were little kids, and we usually walked to school together, picking up Gordie and Charlie along the way.

Mr. O'Dougherty and my dad went out to the yard to look at the wall dividing us from the Bleekers. It had collapsed from the bomb blast. The two bicycles were buried underneath. "I'll have to take the tram to work," said my dad, scratching his head. He had dark brown hair like me, and blue eyes. My mam said I was the dead spit of him. I hoped I wouldn't inherit his temper.

Madeleine said, "Mam and Dad are sending Brensley and Pat back to Edenderry first thing in the morning, Nan."

"They're not!"

"They are, sure. Ireland is safer for them."

"They'll be better out of it right enough," said Mam, shooting Dad a look, "but I don't know about the Ould Sod. Belfast and Dublin will be sure to get it."

Bren looked tired and miserable. Pat wasn't too happy either.

"You'll miss everything," I said. I didn't tell them I'd miss them, too.

Bren shrugged and pulled a face. Pat said, "I don't want to go. I'd rather be blown to fragments than leave England."

"I'll come over later and help ye clean up the soot," Madeleine said to my mam. "All we have is the bit of broken glass. But Mam's upset because St. Theresa fell off the mantelpiece and lost her head. Mam thinks for sure it's a sign."

When they'd gone, I was sent up to bed. They wouldn't let me stay up or help throw the lumps of plaster and broken glass out the window the way they were doing. "It's school for you tomorrow, as usual," said my mam.

The windows in my room were unbroken. But I couldn't sleep. The din of the raid still rang in my ears. My feet were cold. A little bit too early in the year yet for the hot-water bottle and chilblains. I'd left my door open. I could hear my mam and dad arguing; their voices came up the stairs at me like shrapnel. I hated it when they argued.

"If we're to get it, then it's better we all go together." Dad.

". . . whole life in front of him." Mam.

I finally fell asleep.

I couldn't wait to get out of the house in the morning. My dad had gone to work. My mam had cleaned up most of the soot. I didn't even stop for a cup of tea.

"Don't forget your gas mask," said my mam. "Ye'd better start carrying it again. Mr. Clements says for sure the

Jerries'll be dropping the gas on us." Mr. Clements was the butcher. He had opinions on everything. His son Kevin was in my class.

I grabbed my gas mask from out of the shoe cupboard in the hall and ran outside. I scanned the street, looking for damage.

The houses in our neighborhood were all identical: terraced brick, two bedrooms and bathroom up, two rooms down, no basement, freezing in the winter. There was a fireplace for coal or coke, and this provided the only warmth as well as heating the copper tank behind the fireplace for the once-a-week bath. In the summer when you ran the water, it was always cold because nobody kept their fire going, which meant taking cold baths. Outside in the backyard there was a bogs—an outhouse—that you didn't use much in the winter for number two, because if you did you got your bum frozen off. It was fine the rest of the year, though, and had a rich smell of soil, rot, and rust. Toilet paper was a stack of *Liverpool Echo*s, on a wide pine seat that gathered dust and spiders and flakes of rust from the old water tank up in the roof. To flush the tank you pulled the chain, which had a wooden handle polished black through years of use. The houses had no front yards, just a bit of iron railing and a privet hedge: you walked out of your front door and you were on the street. The rent, ten bob a week, was collected every Saturday morning by a man in a greasy black suit who worked for the landlord. We'd never met the landlord: he was like the Holy Ghost, invisible and unknowable.

This morning, the street was full of debris after the raid, everything from bricks, shattered charcoal-colored roof slates, and glass shards from all the broken windows to huge lumps of masonry and chimney pots.

Two houses had been bombed, up near the main road, opposite the Regent Cinema. Good thing they didn't get the Regent: where would I go for my gangster movies! I ran to stare. The fronts of the two houses had been ripped off. I could see the rooms with pictures still on the walls, the fireplaces, the upstairs bathroom with the toilet and bathtub hanging loose. One house had yellow wallpaper upstairs and blue down; the other had pink upstairs and red-and-cream down. The walls and floors had fallen in. I stood in the street for the longest time just staring at them, like God, seeing inside all the rooms at the same time.

An exhausted ARP warden yelled for me to go away.

I couldn't move. Couldn't stop staring.

He came up to me. His face was smudged with soot and grime. "You hard of hearing or what?"

"Was anyone killed?"

"Not here. But you'll be killed if you hang about much longer." He pointed. "Can't you see that whole wall is about to fall down?"

I ran.

I hammered on Bren's door.

His mam came to the door. "Brensley and Pat won't be going to school."

"They're really leaving?"

She nodded.

"How long will they be gone?"

She shook her head and sighed. "I don't know, Jamie. I wish we knew, but we don't."

I passed the bombed houses again. Next to them, on the main road, there was a big billboard, almost as high as the rooftops, that had an old white-haired man in a posh suit. I stopped and stared at it. The old man had a kind face, and was smiling as he held his hands out toward me. PLACE YOURSELF IN OUR HANDS, said the sign. ACME LIFE INSURANCE. It was a wonder the blast from the bombs hadn't blown the old man over.

Bleeker passed me, off to school, with Elsie dragging along behind him. He didn't even look at me. "Move yer legs, worm!" he yelled back at Elsie.

Charlie McCauley's house hadn't been touched. He had his gas mask. I pointed to it. "Whose idea was that? Your mam's, I bet!"

"No, it was me dad. He says I have to carry it now the war's really started. They'll gas us, everyone says so."

I told him about Bren and Pat being sent back to Ireland. He said, "Too bad. They'll miss the best war in history ever. Me dad says it'll be a fight to the finish. There'll be millions dead before it's over, he says." His eyes were searching the ground for shrapnel. He gave an excited yell and picked up a lump from under a privet hedge. He showed it to me. Glistening steel, smooth on two sides, jagged and sharp at the ends. "High-explosive bomb casing," he said, weighing it in his hand. "Must weigh a pound and a half."

"Your mam and dad are not thinking of sending you

away again, are they?" I said. Charlie had been evacuated to Rhyl in North Wales a year ago. He had hated it. He came back in November for a visit and never went back.

Charlie looked shocked. "I hope not. Anyway, I wouldn't go. If they sent me I'd find me way back again."

Charlie had red hair, gingery red, not like Madeleine's, which was a dark fiery-bronze red. He was our leader, sort of. Not that we appointed him leader or anything like that, but we usually did whatever he said because he was braver and crazier than me or Bren or Gordie. It was Charlie who usually decided what we'd do—ride the trams for free by hanging on the back, or sit on the upper deck, out in front in the open-air cage, and yell good words like "piss" and "shit" down at everyone in the street, or go tramping through Childwall Woods—Chilly Woods, we called it—looking for horse chestnuts so we could play conkers, or search for balls on the golf course and sell 'em. He never seemed to run out of ideas of things to do. Which was probably why he got good marks at school: his mind was always on the go.

Gordie was waiting for us at the corner of Broadgreen Road. He wasn't his usual self: he looked pale and sick. And he didn't have his stick. "I'm not coming," he said.

"You're not coming to school?" said Charlie.

Gordie looked at the ground. He shook his head. "I've got to go to me aunt's."

We stared at him.

"And me uncle. They live in Derbyshire. Train's this afternoon. Half-past one."

Charlie said, "That's too bad, Gordie."

"Won't be for long," I said, trying to make him feel better. "War'll be over in a week or two. Our Spitfires and Hurricanes will sort out the Luftwaffe in no time." I went into my imitation of Mr. Churchill's "We shall fight on the beaches . . . we shall never surrender" speech, but my heart wasn't in it. First Bren and Pat, and now Gordie.

Gordie slouched off back home, and we got stopped on St. Oswald Street by a rope barrier and an ARP warden standing outside his sandbagged post. "Unexploded parachute mine," he explained. "You'll have to go round Broadgreen Road."

Parachute mines were the deadliest of the lot because they floated down and went off above ground as soon as they touched a pole or a roof. The blast from them caused the most damage and killed more people.

"Maybe they'll send us all home," said Charlie, "with an unexploded mine so close."

The Broadgreen Road route took us longer than usual because the only way to Snozzy's open to us led us away from the school, then back along Montague Road.

Lots of kids had air-raid stuff they'd picked up on the way to school. Souvenirs. Shrapnel mostly, but other stuff, too, like incendiary fins, cartridge casings, and bits of shot-down barrage balloons. I didn't want to keep shrapnel, but I'd found and kept a short length of green silky rope off a barrage balloon or a parachute mine—I wasn't sure which—because it had a nice feel to it. It was long enough to wrap around my waist a couple of times and tie in the front.

Nobody did schoolwork for the first while. Miss O'Hara let the kids talk about the raid. Several kids were missing, like Bren and Gordie.

Everyone talked at once.

"Anyone killed?"

"The O'Briens were taken off to hospital."

"The Trevors were wiped out. Direct hit."

That stopped us.

"A direct hit!"

"All of them?"

"The whole family."

John Trevor. A year behind us. His older sister, Joan, a year ahead. And their mam and dad. All dead.

We tried to imagine what it would be like to get a direct hit and be dead instead of sitting here in Snozzy's thinking about getting a direct hit and being dead.

"Were they in their shelter?"

Nobody knew.

"Make no difference if they were or not," Two-Ply said. "Get a direct hit and you're gone."

Two-Ply's real name was Max. Last year Annie Tracy, our teacher, asked the class to write on the blackboard as many ideas as they could on the topic of how the school might be improved. Max wrote down only one idea: all the toilets should have two-ply toilet tissue. Everyone called him Two-Ply after that.

We had gas mask drill, the first since Easter. Nobody fooled around the way we used to when we first got the gas masks a year ago, blowing rubber farts out the side of our faceplates, or stumbling about like Frankenstein monsters. Nobody.

The Trevors all dead. Killed by a direct hit.

For the first time since the war started, it was deadly earnest.

FIVE

"I won't go!"

They ignored me.

"Ireland is safe, Nan," said my dad.

"Did Bren and Pat go to Ireland today?" I asked my mam.

"They did."

"Well, I'm not going," I said again. But they carried on arguing over my head.

"Safe, is it!" said my mam. "And them dropping death and destruction on Dublin! If that's safe, then I'm the madwoman right enough!"

"Nan, will ye give over. It was only the one load they dropped, a mistake it was. The pilot thought he was over Liverpool."

"Ha! Only the one load of bombs, was it! How many does it take to kill ye? And what kind of an eejit would mistake Dublin for Liverpool, with a thousand silver balloons like signposts over our heads to show them the way? That was no mistake. Hitler's the divil, and the divil's no fool!"

My dad gave a sigh. "Nan, will ye hush, and not be getting yourself so wrought up." He reached for a Woodbine. "The boy would be as safe in Ireland as any place in the world, don't ye know it well."

You'd think I was invisible. "Look, Dad," I said, "I've no intention—"

"But where would he go in Ireland?" said my mam. "There's no one left in Achill, except Alice, and she's not well enough to take care of a thrush, never mind a lazy lump of a lad twelve years old."

I hated it when they ignored me. And my mam was wrong about me being lazy; I was a slow mover, that was all. And I was no lump either. I was one of the skinniest kids in Snozzy's. And I wasn't really twelve; I'd be thirteen in three weeks.

I felt like screaming at them. Boring Ireland! Boring Wales! The excitement was right here! Leave me be!

My dad lit his Woody. Nobody spoke. I hated them.

When the war broke out a year ago, the government had posters stuck up all over the place: MOTHERS, SEND THEM OUT OF THE CITY they said under a stomach-turning picture of two kids in the countryside. The kids had vomity expressions on their phizogs, a boy and a girl. The boy was older, and he had his arm around the girl's shoulders. Made me want to throw up. Annakin's had one pasted high over the King Edward spuds bin and another above the brussels sprouts: GIVE YOUR KIDS A CHANCE OF GREATER SAFETY AND HEALTH. Cripes! That was when Mam started carrying on to Dad about sending me away.

If Snozzy's kids saw the posters, they tore them down when no one was looking. If they could. I destroyed the ones they had in the post office window and those in the Black Horse, where I went every Friday to get my dad a quart of best bitter beer. I also ripped down the ones in the Old Swan Library at the bottom of Baden Road, our street. But the poster in Costigan's was behind the bacon slicer, and impossible to reach. All I could do was stare, horrified, at the big, razor-sharp wheel and not get too close for fear I would lose my fingers.

Last year, thousands of kids had been evacuated from the cities to rural areas. We called them vackies, short for "evacuees." Charlie McCauley was one of them. He ended up in Wales after Snozzy's organized their own evacuation, the same as lots of other schools did all over England.

I didn't want to go. I told my mam and dad that if they sent me I'd come back on my own, even if it meant walking for twenty hours a day, and dragging myself through hedges of thorns, and sleeping in ditches, even if I starved in the attempt. My dad had laughed and said I didn't need to worry, that we'd all be staying together. "It'd take a lot more than Hitler to break up my family," he'd said.

I remember Charlie going. He was miserable. Half the school went. The teachers lined them all up out in the yard to make sure they had their gas masks and suitcases and a bag lunch for on the train. Then they marched them off to the corner of St. Oswald Street and Prescot Road—Precky Road in Scouse—where five trams waited to take them downtown to the railway station.

They all had labels fixed to their coats and jackets—like rolls of carpet in a warehouse—with their names and addresses on in case anyone got lost.

I waved goodbye to Charlie, but he didn't wave back. Instead he tore his label off and flung it on the ground for dozens of feet to walk over.

I felt sorry for him having to go; he'd miss all the excitement.

Then, just before Christmas, most of them came back, Charlie too, because nothing much was happening: no bombs, no gas, nothing. Except for the food rationing, which started in January, it was like there wasn't a war on at all.

When Charlie came home, some of the other kids laughed and made fun of him. They called him names. "Coward! Scared of the Germans! Sissy! Mam's little baby! Running away!"

I didn't want them calling me names like that.

Up until last night, the war had been a great disappointment to me. No invasion. No mass destruction. And there we'd all been carting these boxed gas masks about with us everywhere we went, even though the only life-threatening gas up to then had been the odd fart rattling around the classroom from Stinky Corcoran, who always smelled like he'd been eating dead vultures.

54

But now things had changed. The war had come to Old Swan.

I'd been looking forward to the war, but hadn't reckoned on losing my pals. I felt let down. Last year I lost my cousin Anthony when Uncle Larry and Auntie Nell sent him to a relative in Ireland. And now Bren and Gordie were gone. And Pat; even though she wasn't exactly a pal, I'd kind of liked having her around.

After dinner that night it was obvious my mam and dad wanted rid of me for a while so they could talk. I didn't want them talking. I knew what they were up to. I saw that look in my mam's eye.

"Ye can go out for a bit, Jamie," she said, "but stay close in case the sirens go."

There came a yell from next door. The Bleekers'. Then another yell, followed by a loud bump.

"Thanks, but I don't want to go out. I'll stay and hear the fight next door."

"Go and take the apple pie to Madeleine. I promised I'd send one over."

She got up and covered the pie with a dish.

The Bleekers were quiet now.

"Don't drop it. Come right back if the alert sounds."

I went down the backyard carrying the pie. The O'Doughertys' yard gate was open, as I expected. I walked up their yard, exactly like ours, past their brick shelter, and knocked on the kitchen door.

Madeleine answered. "Come in, Jamie." She always had a great smile, but tonight it seemed a bit forced.

"Me—*my* mam . . ."

55

"Come in a minute." She took the dish out of my hand.

Her mam and dad were sitting on their sofa, staring into the fire. They looked miserable.

"Nan sent over a pie," said Madeleine.

"That's grand," said Mr. O'Dougherty without looking up.

Mrs. O'Dougherty had dark hair swept back tight from her forehead and tied behind with a rubber band. She always had a laugh on her phizog, but not tonight. Tonight she was staring into the fire like she'd lost something in the red, smoldering coals.

Madeleine put the dish down on the table, then sat on a chair by her mam.

I stood awkwardly by.

Madeleine bounced up again. "I'll make the cup of tea for Jamie."

"No. No thanks. I just had one."

Madeleine sat down. She got up again. "A glass of milk maybe?"

"No thanks, I have to get back."

There came a loud hammering on the front door. "Put that light out!" The ARP warden.

Madeleine's mam and dad didn't move. They stared at the fire.

Madeleine rushed over and closed the hall door to stop the living room light from leaking out into the front, where there was no blackout curtain.

The hammering stopped.

Madeleine let me out the back. "The house is empty without Brensley and Pat," she whispered to me.

I was glad to leave. I'd never known the house so quiet or the O'Doughertys so unhappy. You'd think Bren and Pat had died and gone to hell, or had married Protestants.

My mam and dad were hard at it. I could hear their voices as I came up the back. They stopped when they heard me come in.

Dad was in his chair. Mam was perched on the arm of the sofa. They wasted no time telling me. My heart was sinking before anyone even uttered a word.

"We've talked it over, Jamie," said my mam, "and we've decided."

I looked at my dad. He was mashing his Woody out in the ashtray, avoiding my eyes.

Mam said, "There's a ship sailing tomorrow afternoon, from your dad's dock. We want you to be on it, safe, away from the bombing and the poison gas."

"It'll not be for long," said my dad, looking up at me. "Six months at the most, till the war is over."

I could feel the blood rushing to my head. "What about all that stuff you said last time?" I shouted at my dad. " 'No Hitler will ever break up *my* family,' you said. That's what you said! Don't you remember? Have you—"

"Jamie, hush, will ye," said my mam, "and don't be upsetting yourself—"

"I don't want to go to Ireland. I want to stay here."

"Sure, it's not to Ireland the ship is going," said my mam. "It's Canada."

SIX

"Canada!" I stared at them. "But that's thousands of miles away!"

"There's no war in Canada," Dad said. "Ye'll be safe there."

"I don't want to be safe. I want to stay here with you."

"It's lucky we are to get ye on the ship, so it is," Dad said. "There's hundreds on the Seavac waiting list. The ship was full, but then a couple canceled. It's the grand piece of luck right enough. They sail tomorrow, the twelfth."

"But *Canada*!" I was practically speechless. I hated them. They might just as well have said the moon. What did I know of Canada! Nothing, except it was very large, was colored red on the map, and was the white, frozen part of North America. I'd be alone. Alone on a ship. Alone in a strange country. My mam and dad hated me and I hated them. They wanted rid of me. I could feel my eyes start to well with tears.

My mam reached out, but I flung myself away, and thumped up the stairs.

I didn't sleep.

I was wide awake when the sirens went. I looked at the alarm clock's luminous hands: it was after one.

My mam had come in to see me soon after I had stomped off up the stairs to bed. Trying to make me feel better about sailing off to Canada.

"What part of Canada?" I'd asked her. She didn't know. Could be anywhere.

"It's a big country," I said.

"It is."

"Who would I live with?"

She didn't know the answer to that one either. "But they wouldn't put you in a place you didn't like," she said, stroking my hair. I jerked my head away on the pillow to let her see I wasn't buying any of her blarney, and eventually she let me alone and went back downstairs.

Now the sirens sounded the way I felt: long, low moans swooping over the blacked-out city like all the ghosts of the dead risen from Snozzy's graveyard.

"Jamie!" Mam at the door. "Air raid!"

"I'm coming."

I pulled on pants and jersey, knotted the silky green rope around my waist, and hurried down. For the last time. It was Thursday, the twelfth of September, over an hour past midnight. This was the day that would see me on a ship bound for Canada.

My dad and Mr. O'Dougherty on the back step. Mam in the kitchen with the teapot in her hand, the big brown one she used when there were extra people. Madeleine leaning her backside on the edge of the gas stove, arms folded. They'd been talking, but stopped when I came in.

I could hear Mrs. Bleeker from next door, already in our yard, pushing her kids into our shelter, Elsie whining as usual.

I looked up. Half-moon. Another clear night. No planes yet. Big Nellies high in the sky, moonlit elephants browsing.

"Take this to the shelter." My mam handed me a candle and a box of Swan Vesta matches.

Mrs. Bleeker was talking to my dad in the yard about the terrible bombing in London; she'd heard it on the nine o'clock news.

I set the candle down in the corner of the shelter and lit it. Several chairs were already in place. Elsie sat on one of the chairs, clutching her doll and sucking her thumb as she stared at me. She was still wearing my jersey, the red one a bit short in the sleeves now for me. Bleeker, bruised and glaring, same as last night, said, "What you staring at, Monaghan?"

I didn't know what to say to him, so I said nothing.

Mrs. Bleeker came into the shelter and sat. She opened a shopping bag and took out her knitting. Elsie whined until her mam let her sit on her knee. Once settled, she started swinging the long floppy leg of her doll at her brother's ear. Bleeker grasped the doll by its leg, jerked it quickly out of Elsie's arms, and tossed it at the wall. Elsie screamed, "Tom threw Dolly!"

Bleeker laughed.

"Tom!" said Mrs. Bleeker. "How can you be so—"

"She was kicking me!"

"No I wasn't!"

"Pick it up off the floor," said Mrs. Bleeker.

Bleeker picked it up.

"Now give it back."

Bleeker grinned and gave his sister the doll.

I went out to the yard.

Still quiet. False alarm, probably.

Mam and Madeleine brought tea out to the shelter, and sat with the Bleekers, Mam with her biscuit tin, which she placed down between her feet on the cement floor. Madeleine had a lighted candle in a saucer, which she covered with a clay flower pot and put in the corner next to the other candle. "It'll warm the place a bit," she said.

Mr. O'Dougherty poked his head in the shelter. "Your mam's on her own, Madeleine."

"I'll go right after this cup of tea."

"Bring her over, why don't ye?" said my mam.

"I will," said Madeleine. She skipped down the yard and out the gate.

The night wasn't cold, but Mrs. O'Dougherty wore a fine overcoat, brown maybe, it was hard to tell in the moonlight, with a thick black fur collar that came up high around her neck. With her dark, backswept hair and fur collar she was the fine lady. She sat in the shelter next to

Mrs. Bleeker and took a cup of tea. From where I stood in the yard I could see them all sitting in there.

My mam introduced Bridget O'Dougherty to Mary Bleeker. I couldn't help but notice the difference between the two women: Mrs. O'Dougherty, slim, shining black hair, alert, well dressed; Mrs. Bleeker, heavy, scraggy brown hair, dull-faced, scruffy.

"Did ye have an accident?" Mrs. O'Dougherty said to Bleeker, leaning and peering at his face.

"He was fighting," said Mrs. Bleeker.

"He doesn't have much to say for himself," Madeleine said, smiling.

Bleeker glared at her.

"A false alarm, I'm thinking," said my dad. He and Mr. O'Dougherty had moved from the back step. They now leaned against the shelter, and when they spoke, they turned their heads to the side so their words slid in the open doorway. I stood beside them, watching the sky, and listening to catch the drone of bombers.

"They got away all right, then?" said my mam to Mrs. O'Dougherty.

"They did," said Mrs. O'Dougherty gloomily.

"Ye did the right thing, so ye did," said my mam.

"Ah, we did."

The Irish "dids" like stitches.

"Matt and Bridget sent their two childer back to Ireland," my mam explained to Mrs. Bleeker.

Mrs. Bleeker said, "I wish I could send mine somewhere, so I do."

Silence.

"Maybe the school will organize an evacuation," said my mam, "the same as last year."

"It's not likely, Nan," said Madeleine.

"Jamie's away tomorrow," said my mam. "Today, I mean." She didn't sound happy about it. Which was something.

"Where will he go? Back to Ireland, is it?" said Mrs. Bleeker.

Dad spoke up. "The CORB has a ship leaving in the afternoon for Canada. We're lucky to have Jamie on it. There was a couple of cancellations. Canada will never be attacked. He'll be as safe there as the Pope in Rome."

"What's the CORB?" said Mrs. Bleeker.

"Government-sponsored evacuation," Dad said. "Children's Overseas Reception Board is what the letters stand for."

"It's free, then?" said Mrs. Bleeker.

"It is."

"What about the German U-boats?" said Mrs. O'Dougherty. "Are ye not afraid they'll sink the ship?"

"The ship'll be in a convoy," said my dad, "with a destroyer escort. They'll have no problem with U-boats. If they try anything, the Royal Navy will depth-charge them all to hell."

"Mind your language, Jack," said my mam.

My stomach was in a right twist listening to them talking.

I could hear planes.

"A couple of cancellations ye say, Mr. Monaghan?" said Mrs. Bleeker.

The drone grew louder.

"Do ye think there'd be room for my two?" said Mrs. Bleeker.

"Well now," said my dad, sorry he'd said anything, I could tell from the tone of his voice, "it was the terrible wangle, so it was, getting Jamie on."

Mrs. Bleeker said, "With the baby coming and all, it would be . . ."

I couldn't hear any more because of the noise of the planes. They were almost overhead. The sky was lighting up with flares, just like last night. The anti-aircraft guns started.

"Get inside!" my dad yelled at me, jerking a thumb at the shelter.

The shelter was crowded with us all in there. The women moved the chairs back to make room for us. Dad pulled the tarpaulin door cover closed so the light wouldn't show. The candle blew out. I couldn't see anything. I groped in my pocket for the matches, found them, and relit the candle.

"Good boy," said my dad.

"It would be the best thing for Tom and Elsie," said Mrs. Bleeker. "To get away from . . ." She stopped and started to cry. ". . . from . . ."

Silence except for the noise outside and snuffles from Mrs. Bleeker.

Dad handed her his handkerchief. "It's hardly used," he joked feebly. She took it and held it to her face.

Elsie, on her knee, clung tightly to her, one arm about her mother's neck and the other about her doll.

"Where's your—where's Mr. Bleeker?" said my dad.

Mrs. Bleeker didn't answer. She shook her head.

Nobody spoke.

Then Mrs. O'Dougherty started saying something to my mam in a low voice, and my mam started nodding. I couldn't hear what was said because Elsie was jerking her doll about like a puppet and talking in a high piping voice to her brother. "Dolly velly solly she kick Tom-Tom, Dolly velly velly solly."

Bleeker ignored both sister and doll. I watched from the corner of my eye, pretending I had seen and heard nothing. I was enjoying the expression on Bleeker's face. It was hard to tell for sure with all those bruises, but he looked embarrassed.

"Tom-Tom?" Tiny squeak of a voice. Doll thrust forward into Bleeker's face. "Dolly velly solly?"

Bleeker gave a growl like a lion, taking the doll's arm in his teeth in a pretend bite, and Elsie screamed with delight, pulling her doll away from the jaws of the lion. "Arrrrgh! Arrrrgh!" roared the lion. "No! No! No!" cried Elsie, squealing and giggling and wriggling on her mother's lap.

"Stop it, you two!" said Mrs. Bleeker, knitting held high.

I listened to the noise outside. Whistles. The bombs were starting. High explosives, like last night.

Crump! Sounded close, but the shelter didn't shake.

My dad pulled the tarpaulin aside and peered out. I dropped on my knees and squinted out from the bottom. The sky was alight again with flares, like last night. A fat

65

lot of good it was, the blackout, when the Germans could find the city so easily in the moonlight, and then drop flares to light their target.

I thought about the Trevors all killed by a direct hit. "Get a direct hit and you're gone," one of the kids had said. He was right. If they dropped a bomb in our yard we were all gone, Monaghans, O'Doughertys, Bleekers, every one of us, shelter or no shelter. I wanted to be outside. No matter that flying shrapnel and debris would more than likely kill me, I didn't want to die in a brick tomb.

I crawled out under the tarpaulin on my knees into the yard. The high whining scream of a bomb made me cover my ears. I felt a hand on my collar as I was dragged back into the shelter.

My dad. "Is it mad ye are?" He threw me back. I almost fell over Bleeker.

"Sit here, Jamie," said my mam, getting up for me to sit in her chair, "and don't move from there!"

I looked at Bleeker. He was staring at me. What was he thinking? That I was scared? Well, he'd be right. I was scared of dying from a direct hit in that airless concrete trap.

My dad started to say something to me, but a sudden violent explosion made the earth shake. My ears rang with the noise of it.

"Holy Lord Jesus!" my mam said.

"Sweet Mother of Mercy!" said Mrs. O'Dougherty.

"That was close!" Mrs. Bleeker.

The noise had deafened me a bit; I couldn't hear them properly.

Then came another explosion, a bit farther away. Crump! This time I felt only a tremor. Then different sounds: a rain of debris, and a noise that reminded me of Indian arrows as they shot away from the bow in Hollywood Westerns. Close-up of fist holding bow. Fingers release feathered arrows. One, two, three. *Phwumph! Phwumph! Phwumph!* Cut to palefaces pierced, clutching, and dying.

Quiet. All the planes had passed over.

Ambulance and fire truck sirens wailing along Precky Road.

"Would ye see what ye can do?" said Mrs. Bleeker, touching the sleeve of my dad's cardigan.

"Huh?"

"The children and the ship."

"I will, then," said my dad. "But I can promise nothing."

We waited for the planes to come back, but they didn't come. Must have circled away in some other direction. Dad pushed the tarpaulin open.

Bright orange glow.

"Come quick!" my dad yelled.

I tumbled out behind him.

Our house was on fire.

SEVEN

We all stood for a moment in the yard, gaping up at the flames and smoke leaping from the broken window of my room at the back of the house.

My mam was the first to move. "Get the bucket from under the sink, Jack!" she yelled.

The O'Doughertys and the Bleekers hurried off to their own homes.

Except for the short length of hose that came with the ARP stirrup pump there was no hosepipe. The only hoses I'd ever seen, apart from those used by the fire department, were the ones in the posh houses by the Sefton Park golf course where the toffs—rich people—used them to wash their cars.

I followed my dad and mam into the house. My dad snatched the bucket from under the sink while I grabbed the one we kept in the hall with the stirrup pump. "Fill yours from the bathroom, Jamie," Mam said, taking the pump.

We rushed up the stairs. The bathroom was off the landing. I hurried in through the smoke and pushed the bucket under the tap. The smoke made me cough, like the time I tried smoking one of my dad's Woodbines. Water pounded and splashed into the bucket.

I hauled the water up the three steps to the top landing, and into my smoke-filled room, almost tripping and spilling it over a small heap of clothing that my mam must have snatched from my wardrobe. Dad had already filled his bucket downstairs, and was pumping while Mam directed the hose nozzle at the flames. My bed was on fire. And the floor. I put down my bucket, waited until Dad had emptied the first one, then took the empty bucket to the bathroom and refilled it.

"Give it here!" It was Mr. O'Dougherty, back again. He took my full bucket, and handed back an empty one. "Stay and fill the buckets," he said, rushing off. I'd no sooner filled it than Madeleine was there with another empty one. "Good lad, Jamie!" she cried, like she was enjoying herself. Mrs. O'Dougherty had a bucket, too. There were plenty of buckets now; I just couldn't fill them fast enough as I knelt in the bathtub, coughing and choking from the smoke. Someone, Mr. O'Dougherty probably, was down in the kitchen filling buckets, for I could hear the constant pounding of feet up and down the stairs.

The Bleekers came back. Mrs. Bleeker said, "Can I . . . ?"

"There's enough help," said Mrs. O'Dougherty with a look at Mrs. Bleeker's swollen belly. "Go on home with ye and the childer. We've got this under control, so we have."

I was sure I'd filled a hundred buckets and swallowed a ton of soot by the time the all-clear sounded. My arms ached and my legs were soaked.

It took ages, but finally the fire was out.

We all stood in my room, our faces and hands and clothing black with smoke. Bleeker, too: he had stayed to help, probably because his mam ordered him to. The room was no longer a room but a black husk. I could see, in the light from the landing, black, charred remains of furniture, my bed, wardrobe, chest of drawers. The floor was burned through. Everything sopping wet. The water had gone downstairs into the living room.

And my comics. I'd kept them in a big cardboard box in the bottom of the wardrobe. They had all burned to nothing. My *Hotspurs*! It had taken years to collect them. All the others had gone, too, *Wizards*, *Rovers*, *Adventures*. There must have been a hundred of them, all gone.

"Your room is destroyed, Jamie," said my dad, shaking his head.

I felt Bleeker watching me.

The dead incendiary bomb with its green fin lay on the floor over near the wall. I looked up at the hole in the ceiling and roof where the bomb had arrowed through. I stared again at my room, unable to tear my eyes away from the blackness I saw there, for it mirrored perfectly the blackness I felt inside.

. . .

I went to my bunk under the stairs, but slept very little, listening to my mam and dad sweeping and bailing out water from downstairs, and thinking about my ruined room upstairs, the black, sopping house, Mam and Dad left on their own, and the ship.

The ship.

Waiting for me down at the dock.

Waiting to take me away from Mam and Dad, my friends, Snozzy's, everything I knew, everything I'd grown up with in Liverpool since I'd come from Ireland seven years ago when I was only six.

What if I skipped off the ship just before it sailed? I imagined myself hurrying down the gangway in the dark when no one was looking. Where would I stay? What would I do for food? And money? All I had in my Crawford's Cream Crackers tin was one pound and ten shillings, which I'd been saving toward a new bike. I couldn't come home again, not after skipping ship, they'd be mad at me. And then they'd send me to Ireland or Wales or Scotland anyway. I couldn't win.

Yells from the Bleekers next door. The husband must be back. A couple of loud thumps, like chairs falling, then silence.

Mrs. Bleeker came in the back door. I could hear her talking to Mam and Dad, but couldn't hear what they were saying, just a few words—Tom moving, or Tom and the movies.

Movies. I loved them. Gangster movies were my favorite. James Cagney was the best of them all. Then

George Raft, and then Humphrey Bogart. Cagney was terrific as Rocky in *Angels with Dirty Faces*. I felt so sorry for Rocky at the end I just about cried, but managed to keep it in by biting my lips real hard. Charlie and Gordie and Bren would have wet themselves laughing if they'd seen me crying. The same in *Each Dawn I Die*. They shot Raft. I hated that. I loved him so much. In *The Roaring Twenties*, Cagney ended up dying on the church steps. The woman said to the policeman, "This is Eddie Bartlett. He used to be a big shot." I could have wept my eyes out it was so sad. But I didn't. They were tough, and so was I. I bit my lip so hard when Eddie died I drew blood. I could taste it, salty on my tongue. It didn't bother me.

Before I dropped off to sleep I imagined that the ship went to Hollywood. My parents didn't want me, but Warner Bros. needed me for a movie with Cagney, Raft, and Bogart. The movie was called *Son of Eddie*. I was the son. I was an even bigger tough guy than my dad, Eddie, who had died outside on the church steps. I never bothered to write to my real dad or mam, and I never saw them again: it served them right; they shouldn't have sent me away.

My dad had already gone to work when I woke up. It was late, eleven o'clock.

The place was a mess. My mam looked like she hadn't slept. She had a small suitcase packed.

"Is that for me?"

"It is so. It was your dad's. The smoke has almost everything destroyed, including your good gray trouser. Ye'll have to wear them ye have on. I washed your other few things the best I could."

"Mam?"

"Hmmmn?"

"I don't want to go."

"I know, Jamie, but it's for the best. It'll not be for long, ye'll see."

"I hate you! I don't want to go."

"Your dad will be back for ye in his lunch hour. There won't be much time. He's going to try and get the Bleeker childer on the ship if he can. They're to be ready, too. If he can't manage it—well, they'll stay where they are, I suppose."

"The Bleekers!"

That thumb-sucking whiny little girl, and her tough scruffy brother! Who needed them! If there was space on the ship, why hadn't Dad gone around to Charlie's house and asked Mr. McCauley if they wanted to send Charlie? It all wouldn't be so bad if Charlie could come. I should have thought of it myself. Now it was too late.

"Eat this," said my mam. "It's the last bit of food ye'll get for a while."

I sat down to a cup of tea, a dried-egg omelette stiff as a place mat, a sausage filled with the sawdust from Mr. Clements's floor, and a slice of fried bread, not done on both sides the way I liked it.

"Sorry there isn't the bit of bacon," said Mam, "but we've had our ration for the week. I'll do ye another piece of bread if ye like."

"No."

"Ye're not taking that lump of rope with ye, I hope. Your blazer won't button properly."

I looked down at my new belt. "It's mine. I'll take what I like." I knew I was acting like a twerp, but I didn't care. "And my blazer stinks."

"Ah, it's the smoke. It needs cleaning, so it does."

The taxi came up to the front door. My dad got out. He was in his working clothes: brown cords, collarless shirt, boots, cloth cap. He looked tired.

"Are ye ready, Jamie? Then get in."

Mrs. Bleeker came to her door and stood, saying nothing. I could see her two kids in the gap behind her.

"Get in, missus," my dad said to her.

"God bless ye," said Mrs. Bleeker, stepping aside to let her kids out to the street.

I'd never been in a taxi before. It was crowded. Dad sat up front with the driver while the rest of us sat in the back, the Bleekers in one seat, me and my mam facing them in the other. Mrs. Bleeker looked awful, pinched and pale. She had a cardboard box on her knee, tied with string. My mam reached over and pressed her hand.

Bleeker looked mean, as usual, but that could have just been the bruises, or it might have been my own fear of him; who knows, maybe he looked normal when his face wasn't so battered. I examined his face, trying to guess what he was thinking, but I couldn't tell how he felt, couldn't tell if he wanted to go on the ship or not. He stared out the window the whole way.

Elsie, too, was silent, clutching her doll in one arm and the sleeve of her mam's coat with the other.

We drove right up to the gangway, and all got out. There was a crowd at the gangway. Dad paid the driver. The taxi drove away, past a bombed warehouse, through heaps of debris scattered over the dockside.

I'd always liked the docks: smells of the sea, and tar and creosote. But not today. Misery was all I could smell today. I looked up at the ship. It was huge. Two funnels. I read the name on the ship's prow: *City of Benares*. Stupid name for a ship, calling it after a city, a city in India, sounded like.

"Say goodbye to your mother, Jamie," Dad said. "We'll have to be quick, they're about to raise the gangway. I'll come up onto the deck with ye."

Mam was crying. She handed me the suitcase, then squashed me in her arms, hanging on to me. She smelled of soot and lavender water. I wanted to cry, too, but I didn't because it was all her fault.

I could hear Elsie, carrying on behind me, bawling. Her mam said, "Mind what I said, Tom. Take care of your sister. Stay together, ye hear?"

Bleeker said nothing. He was looking down at the ground and kicking the dirt with his shoes.

"Ye hear me, Thomas?" said Mrs. Bleeker, catching him by the shoulders with both hands.

Bleeker mumbled something.

"Look at me, Thomas."

Bleeker raised his head and looked at his mother.

Mrs. Bleeker said nothing, just looked at him, then

pushed his hair off his forehead, touched his bruised face with the backs of her fingers, gently, like he was made of glass, and kissed him quickly on the cheek.

I pulled away from my mam, and started up the gangway with my dad. A man at the foot of the gangway said, "You there! You can't board now, we're—"

But my dad took no notice. "Come on, Jamie."

"We'll write ye a letter every week," Mam called. "But write as soon as ye get there, and send us the address, d'ye hear me, Jamie?"

I couldn't speak.

The deck was crowded with people, kids mostly. Dad put his arms around me in an awkward hug. Hugging was something we just never did. He smelled of stale cigs. "Be the good boy, Jamie. Be strong. Don't let me down. Look on it as a holiday. I wish it was myself could take the six-month holiday in Canada."

The two Bleeker kids were behind him, at the rail, almost lost in the crowd of kids. Elsie was crying still, clutching her doll and waving down to her mam. Bleeker didn't wave. He looked even meaner and tougher than usual.

"Ye'll write every week once ye're settled? Your mam will worry if ye don't."

I nodded.

"Promise?"

I nodded again.

He gave me a leather wallet, new. "It's for your birthday."

I stared at the wallet.

"Look inside."

I put my suitcase down on the deck and opened the wallet. There was money, a ten-bob note, enough for a week's rent on our house. And a card with my name and address behind a cellophane window. But I didn't care about it. "Thanks, Dad."

"Ye'll be thirteen. A man should have a wallet. Keep it in your trouser. It's your pocket money for three months. I'll send more if ye're there any longer than that."

"What if you and Mam are killed by the gas and the bombs?"

"Your mother and I are well able to take care of ourselves. Hitler isn't going to get us, I promise. We'll be here when ye get back."

A woman was waiting.

"This is Miss Fisher," said my dad. "She'll be in charge till ye're handed over to someone in Canada." He said to the woman, "This is Jamie." He rested a hand on my shoulder. "And the other two childer." He jerked his head. "The Bleekers, Tom and Elsie."

Miss Fisher smiled and said hello. She had a posh voice, like Alvar Lidell, the man who read the BBC news.

I gave her the once-over, the way Cagney or Bogart would. Younger than my mam, she was about Madeleine's age, friendly smile. Ready to hate her, too, I didn't smile back.

A loud rasping bellow from one of the ship's funnels made me jump. They were raising the gangway.

"Goodbye, Jamie!" Dad turned and ran back down the gangway.

I pushed into the crowd of kids at the side of the ship and looked down in time to see him leap onto the dock from the ascending gangway, already several feet in the air. He fell to his knees, sprang up, and turned and waved. Mam was waving, too. What if I never saw them again, never? I waved reluctantly back. The crowd of parents on the dockside waved and called out.

It all made me think of *Shipyard Sally*, a movie I saw with Charlie and the others: Gracie Fields was singing her famous "Wish Me Luck" hit while hundreds of people stood on the dockside waving the troops goodbye as they left for battle overseas. Then a chorus of what sounded like a thousand voices thundered the song from the silver screen. "Wish Me Luck," they sang as they waved goodbye. Lots of people in the Regent were crying real tears, and then the whole audience started singing "Wish Me Luck." What a thundering row!

The only difference now was I couldn't see hundreds of people madly waving, nor could I hear any stirring, patriotic music. All I could see below was a bunch of mams and dads waving their hands and weeping into their handkerchiefs. It would serve them right if they never saw any of us ever again. I hated them.

The ship pulled away from the dock. I looked down at the sea. We were very high. The gap grew wider. Soon my mam and dad and all the other people were only blobs in the distance. Many of the little kids were crying.

I picked up my suitcase and followed Miss Fisher along the swaying deck.

EIGHT

Bleeker followed behind carrying his cardboard box by its string in one hand and holding his sister's hand with the other. Which was a change from the usual "Move yer legs!" the times she trailed along behind him.

I turned and looked back, but couldn't see the people on the dock, only the tall Royal Liver Building and its blue Liver Birds on the top.

Miss Fisher led us toward the back of the ship in the bright afternoon sun, the wind from the mouth of the river Mersey strong in our phizogs. She stopped at a stairway. "This deck we're standing on is called the main deck," she said with a smile. "Each deck has a different name, all right?"

We stared at her. She reminded me of Miss O'Hara.

"All right?" Miss Fisher said again.

Me and Bleeker said nothing; Bleeker scowled at her,

but Elsie nodded dutifully, clutching her doll to her chest.

Fish 'n' Chips walked up the steps. I was right behind her. She was wearing a brown wool coat, and slacks—like one of those land girls, so called because they helped the war effort by planting potatoes and cleaning out pigsties—so there wasn't any leg for me to see. She stopped at the top and waited for us to catch up. Her shoulder-length brown hair was blowing into her eyes. She was like a British film star, like Margaret Lockwood in *The Lady Vanishes*—that was a smashing movie. Gordie had paid his way into the Regent and then, when the usher had his back turned, let me and Charlie and Bren in the side door.

"This is called the *upper* deck," Miss Fisher said in her nice shiny voice. "Over here is the dining room. It's a super ship. You'll love it." We followed her through a door. The dining room was long, with pale blue table-cloths, black polished high-back chairs, and gleaming silver. There were flowers in vases on the tables. It was like being in a movie. Miss Fisher led us outside again, and we climbed another stairway. The ship looked new, every-thing neat and bright, not a bit like the old tub I always sailed on with my mam and dad to Dublin in the sum-mer holidays. The *Benares* was no ordinary ship, I could see; it was a posh luxury liner meant for toffs.

Up the stairs again. "This third deck is the promenade deck. There's one last deck above this one, the boat deck; you can explore that one for yourselves. This one, the promenade deck, is the one I want to show you today."

She held a door open for us. We stepped over a sill and were inside a big room painted yellow. Several kids, sitting around playing board games, looked up as we came in. Miss Fisher sat on the edge of an easy chair. The square shoulder pads in her coat moved up to her ears. She wriggled and pulled the coat down. The wind had made her cheeks pink. She had gray-green eyes. We sat opposite on a sofa. The furniture was all new, and rich-looking.

"Sorry to sound like a tour guide, but one of my jobs is to teach you where everything is." She smiled. "This is the playroom. It's also the muster station for our group. Which means this is the place you come to if there's an emergency. Right here in this area where we are now. That's why I wanted to show it first."

"What kind of an emergency?" said Bleeker, scowling.

"Enemy attack usually, that kind of thing. You'll hear the PA telling you to go to your muster station."

"What kind of attack?" said Bleeker.

"Enemy dive bombers—Stukas. Or U-boats. We're not expecting any attacks, though, because our ship will be in a convoy of many ships, all protected by the navy. But when there's a lifeboat drill, this is the place you come to, all right?"

We stared.

"You will see me here with the rest of the group, sixteen of us altogether."

Elsie sucked her thumb.

"Super," said Miss Fisher.

Elsie started whining in a tiny voice. "Want my mam. Wanna go home."

But Miss Fisher had already bounced up and gone to a cupboard. While her back was turned, Bleeker grabbed his sister's doll and kicked it like a football. The doll sailed high in the air and landed on a snakes and ladders board. Elsie screamed. The two girls playing snakes and ladders screamed. Elsie ran across the room to recover her doll. The two girls glared at us.

Miss Fisher brought back an armful of life jackets from the cupboard and stood waiting for Elsie to return.

"Tom kicked Dolly!" Elsie whined.

Miss Fisher looked sympathetic, but handed out the life jackets in a no-nonsense manner. "Put these on, and keep them on all the time, it's the rule. You take them off only to eat and sleep, but even then they must be close to you."

She gave us orange-colored life jackets. "Put Dolly down on the table for just a minute, Elsie, that's it. Also, when you go to bed at night, you must keep your clothes on."

"What! Wear my coat and keks in bed? Not me!" said Bleeker.

Keks were trousers in Scouse.

"Captain's orders," said Miss Fisher. "Everyone sleeps in their day clothes in case there's an emergency during the night."

When we'd struggled into the life jackets, Miss Fisher said, "I'll take you below again, to your cabins." Down we went. "Don't forget the four decks," she said, leading the way. "Main deck for cabins; upper deck for dining room; promenade deck for emergencies, in the play-room; and the boat deck is on the top, all right?"

But I was only half listening as I thought about the way Bleeker had kicked his sister's doll, and I wished again that it was Charlie who was with me, or Bren, or Gordie.

This time, when we stepped inside off the main deck, it was into a narrow corridor with cabins. Miss Fisher stopped at cabin 11. "Which side of the ship are we on, left or right?"

"Right," I said, forgetting to work on my hatred. Maybe she actually was a teacher. She sure sounded like one.

"What is the right side of a ship called?" she said to Bleeker.

He scowled at her.

"The right is the starboard," I said, "and the left is the port side." I couldn't help showing off sometimes. Besides, I wanted to get the lectures over with; I was starting to feel hungry.

Two girls pushed past us. "Hello, Miss Fisher." They looked about ten or eleven.

Fish 'n' Chips gave them one of her nice smiles. "Hello, Theresa, Laura. Quite right, Jamie. Starboard right, port left."

Bleeker must have been reading my mind. He said, "When do we eat?"

"Lunch is over," said Miss Fisher, "and dinner isn't for hours. But I'll ask the galley—that's the kitchen—if they can find you something."

83

She pushed open the door of number 11. I looked in. It was tiny. There was an electric light switch on the wall beside the door. I clicked it. A light came on in the ceiling. I clicked it off. The light went out. My own electric light. Astounding! I'd never lived in a room with electric light before. Lots of houses in Liverpool had the electric, but our house in Baden Road must have been built when Henry the Eighth was a boy. I was only used to pulling down a chain that turned on the gas, and then I would light the mantle with a match.

Miss Fisher said, "Tom and Jamie, this cabin's yours. Two berths, an upper and a lower. You can decide who gets to sleep where. Leave your bags. Then I'll take you to see Elsie's cabin."

"She stays with me," said Bleeker, dropping his cardboard box onto the cabin floor. He sounded like Edward G. Robinson. "Me an' my sister bags this cabin."

"Sorry," said Miss Fisher, "but boys go with boys and girls with girls, it's the rule."

"I don't care about the rule," said Bleeker. "My mam says she stays with me."

I expected Fish 'n' Chips to start getting upset, but she didn't. She smiled at Bleeker as though he was her favorite son, took Elsie's hand, and headed down the corridor. "Elsie wants to be with the other girls, don't you, Elsie?"

Elsie nodded solemnly and looked back at her brother. "I want to be with the other girls, Tom."

Bleeker followed angrily down the corridor after his

sister. I dropped my suitcase onto the cabin floor beside Bleeker's box and traipsed after them.

"This side of the ship is boys," said Miss Fisher over her shoulder as we followed along. "The girls are all on the other side, the port side. Boys on the starboard, girls on the port, got it?"

We made a turn along another corridor. I had noticed by now that the crew seemed to be all dark-skinned men from India, wearing turbans on their heads and sandals on their bare feet. They glided silently by us in the corridor. It was a bit scary. I knew nothing about Indians from India except they turned up in movies sometimes, mysterious, magical, sleeping on beds of nails, sitting cross-legged on carpets and playing funny-looking pipes to charm snakes out of bowls, or climbing ropes and disappearing into the sky.

I reckoned we were now at the stern of the ship. One of the Indian men came out of a cabin, nodded and smiled at Miss Fisher, and went on his way.

"These are all crew cabins," said Miss Fisher.

We turned right into another long corridor. We stopped. "Elsie is in 14"—Miss Fisher knocked on the door—"with Patricia Richers."

The door was opened by a tall girl with hair the color of straw. She was older, about fifteen or sixteen, I reckoned. She smiled when she saw Elsie, and stood back for her to enter. "Welcome," she said with a laugh. "Step into my castle, little princess." She had a cockney accent: for "castle" she said "car-sl," and for "little" she said "li-il."

"This is Patricia," Miss Fisher said to Elsie. "You're in her cabin. Patricia will take care of anything you need."

Elsie went inside and looked around. "Which bunk is mine?"

She didn't look much like a princess in her scuffed, broken shoes, faded blue hand-me-down coat, and tearstained face.

"Which one would you like?" said Patricia.

Elsie pointed to the upper berth. "That one."

"Then it's yours," said Patricia.

Bleeker watched and listened. He seemed uncertain, wondering, it seemed, whether to leave his sister with this stranger.

Elsie smiled, which she didn't do often. She was almost pretty if you ignored her butchered hair. She seemed to have taken an instant liking to Patricia.

"What's your dolly's name, then?" said Patricia.

"Dolly."

" 'Aven't you got no suitcase, then?"

"This is Elsie's brother, Tom," said Miss Fisher. "He will bring his sister's things over later, won't you, Tom."

Patricia smiled at Bleeker. She had a thin beak of a nose, blue eyes set close together, and a way of craning her head when she spoke that made me think of a bird.

Bleeker shrugged. Patricia didn't seem to notice the cuts and bruises on his face.

"Patricia will bring Elsie up to the muster station at mealtimes and whenever there's a drill," Miss Fisher said to Bleeker. "Your sister is in super hands." She smiled.

"I'll leave you all to settle into your cabins while I go have a word with the cook."

I decided to find my way back to the cabin on the outside of the ship instead of walking back through the narrow passageways like a rabbit in a burrow. I stepped out onto the portside deck and headed aft—I remembered that's what they call the stern of a ship.

Bleeker came fast behind me. Maybe he thought I was trying to grab the top bunk for myself. Maybe I was.

"Hey! Monaghan!"

I stopped.

Bleeker came up to me. From the scowl on his face I thought he was about to punch me. I didn't want to let him see that he scared me, so I put on my most bored expression and waited.

But he didn't want to punch me. He pointed toward the land. "See that?"

I looked. We were in the middle of the river, about opposite the Wallasey pier. "See what?"

"We're not moving."

He was right. The ship had stopped.

We leaned over the side of the ship, looking to see if there was something in the way. I heard a loud rattling noise from up front.

"They're dropping anchor," said Bleeker. "Hey!" He turned to a passing crewman. "Why we stopping?"

The man didn't seem to know English. Not Bleeker's anyway. He shook his head. "Sorry."

An English crewman, an officer, a tall thin man in a

navy blue uniform, saw us and came over. "Can I be of help?" He had a black beard.

"Why we stopped?" said Bleeker roughly.

"Mines," said the officer. "The Luftwaffe sewed up the mouth of the river with the blighters. We shan't be sailing until they're all cleaned up."

"When will that be?" demanded Bleeker.

"Tomorrow. In the afternoon probably."

When the officer had gone, Bleeker grabbed my arm. "You know what that means, don't you, Monaghan?"

I didn't like him grabbing my arm. I shook myself free. "No, what?"

Bleeker's scowl disappeared.

Because his face was usually tightly clenched, I'd never really noticed his eyes properly before. They were blue, I could see now, a light clear blue, like the blue of a robin's egg.

"It means we'll be sailing on Friday the thirteenth!" he said.

NINE

"Toss you for it, then." I took a penny from my pocket and balanced it on my thumbnail. "Heads or tails?"

"Don't want to toss for it. Top bunk's mine."

"But that's not fair. You can't claim something's yours just like that."

"Yes I can. Top one's mine." Bleeker climbed up the ladder and sat on the edge of the bunk. "I'm on it. It's mine."

I bounced the coin in my hand. "Fate will decide."

"No it won't."

"I'm surprised, you being superstitious—all that Friday the thirteenth stuff—that you'd want to sleep on the top. Everyone knows how unlucky the top is."

"No it's not."

"This is how fights start." I was trying to be reasonable.

"Ye want to fight for it?" Bleeker stared down at me.

"I thought you said you don't believe in fighting, that people shouldn't fight."

"It's the same as fighting Hitler," said Bleeker. "Sometimes you gotta fight for what's yours, even when you don't want to."

"But that bunk isn't yours!"

"Yes it is."

I didn't care enough about the bunk to fight for it. But I couldn't let Bleeker bully me and get away with grabbing the best bunk without some sort of protest. If I did, he'd soon be ordering me about and I'd be his monkey for the rest of the voyage. I had my pride. On the other hand, the last thing I wanted was a fight with him. He could beat me. I knew it, and he knew it.

"I'll fight if I have to," I said. "But all I'm asking for is fair treatment. So let's toss a coin."

"No."

I took a deep breath. "Then it'll have to be a fight."

"Ye want to fight me?"

"No, I don't, but you leave me no choice." I took off my life jacket and my school blazer with its cap rolled up in the pocket. "Come on, let's get it over with."

Bleeker's eyes narrowed to slits. "Where? Ye want to fight in here?"

"Course not. There's no room. We can go out on the deck."

Bleeker hesitated. My heart was thumping. I'd try to get in a couple of good punches at least before he made me throw in the towel.

There came a knock at the door. I opened it.

A smiling Miss Fisher handed me a brown paper bag. "Sandwiches. I hope you two like roast beef. There's a couple of apples, too."

"Thanks." I hadn't had much roast beef since food rationing started. Anything worth eating was rationed: butter, eggs, cheese, jam, sugar, even sweets—candy. We got a mingy little piece of meat each week, hardly enough to keep a cat alive, never mind a family, and the dried eggs and powdered potatoes tasted like rat shit. But the thought of having to fight Bleeker took the good out of a roast beef feast. I was no longer hungry.

Fish 'n' Chips held up a second, smaller, bag. "I'll take this over to Elsie." She pointed to a wardrobe. "There's a laundry bag in there. Put your dirty linen in it. A steward comes by, cleans the cabin, and picks up the laundry every day. If your shoes need cleaning, just leave them outside the door."

"Thanks." I started to close the door.

"Jamie."

"Yes?"

"Try to remember the rules."

"Rules?"

"Life jackets stay on, remember?" She nodded at Bleeker. "Like Tom."

Bleeker grinned.

"I'll remember." I closed the door.

"I'll remember," Bleeker mimicked.

"Shut up, Bleeker!"

"This is the life!" said Bleeker. "Plenty to eat, and they clean your shoes and do your laundry." He rubbed his hands together. "And do try to remember the super rules, Monaghan," he finished in a poor imitation of Fish 'n' Chips's voice.

"Up yours!" I said.

"Let's eat." Bleeker sat at the tiny table, his eyes on the brown bag in my hand.

I held the bag behind my back. "No. First things first. We've got to fight, remember? We can eat after."

"Eat now. Fight later."

"No."

"You'll feel stronger after you've eaten," said Bleeker.

"I'll throw up all over you."

Bleeker stared at me. I could see he was thinking hard. "Tell you what," he said after a while, "I'll arm-wrestle you for top bunk."

"Arm-wrestle?" Why hadn't I thought of that? Arm-wrestling wasn't the same as fighting, but it was just as good a way of settling an argument. It was actually better, for you didn't have to be fast and skillful, and it did no damage to your eyes and teeth and lips. "Okay, if you like," I agreed, trying to sound like it didn't much matter to me how we settled it.

"Two out of three wins," said Bleeker.

Bleeker took off his life jacket and the oversized coat jacket, and we squatted beside the table, elbow to elbow, and clasped and pressed and strained and grunted for several minutes.

I knew I was strong from all my work on the monkey bars. Every day after school me and Charlie and Bren and Gordie went to the Albany Street playground and spent most of our time there on the bars, swinging and climbing and doing tricks. I expected to win.

But Bleeker was strong, and as in the fight with Stinky Corcoran, he didn't give up easily. I had his arm back within a few inches of the tabletop when he let out a piercing scream that scared me half to death and he forced my arm up and down. I couldn't believe it. I'd thought for sure I had him. My knuckles hit the table. Crash! I really hated him at that moment.

"First down to me," said Bleeker, grinning triumphantly.

"Screaming's against the rules."

"I didn't scream—yelled, that's all."

He wouldn't fool me so easily next time. I gripped his hand and applied the pressure. He was still grinning at me. This time I'd tire him out by keeping a steady sixty-degree strain of hatred on him. I'd wipe that superior grin off his ugly face. I bunched up over my biceps and gradually forced his arm over about sixty degrees or so. Then I kept it there. He wasn't grinning now. I could see a pearl of sweat on his forehead.

Our arms began a tremor. He tried to push his arm upright, but I gritted my teeth and held firm, not trying for a down, merely holding. I could feel the sweat trickle behind my ear. My biceps felt like a balloon. I waited him out, patient, unyielding.

When at last he yelled and tried to flip my arm over the way he had before, it didn't work. I'd worn him down;

his strength had gone. I withstood the rush, and as soon as I felt his weakness, I pushed his arm down flat onto the table. "We're even," I gasped.

He stood, and started leaping about the cabin, uttering wild whoops, and massaging his sore muscles. He frightened me with the noise. I thought he'd gone mad. Then he crouched and leaped again, whooping like a Hollywood Indian.

"Are you all right?" I shouted at him.

Instead of answering me, he flung himself about the small cabin, whooping, arms whirling, and it made me think of Charlie and the bat we found one time in an old abandoned stone cottage on the edge of Chilly Woods. Bren was there, too. The bat whirled and swooped about the empty cottage, emitting tiny squeaks, while Charlie chased and slashed at it with a tree branch, trying to kill it so he could see it close up. "Leave it go," said Bren. "Don't hurt it." But I figured the bat was doomed: once Charlie made up his mind, it was usually hard to get him to change it. The bat flew about erratically up high in the roof. Charlie yelled and slashed, jumping up to reach it. Then the bat flew out of one of the open windows and was gone. Charlie cursed. Bren looked at me and grinned.

Bleeker swooped about the cabin like that bat; you'd think he was being pursued by the devil himself.

Suddenly he stopped and sat cross-legged on the floor, muttering wildly to himself. It was Latin from the Mass, for I heard a familiar *"Et resurrexit tertia die, secundum scripturas"* in there somewhere. Plus a bunch of other stuff.

Then he got up and kneeled, like he was about to pray, his elbow in position on the table. He glared at me, blue eyes now like ice, wanting to kill me. Scary he was. That wild and crazy performance had been for my benefit, I was certain; he was trying to scare the shit out of me.

But I shrugged my shoulders a few times to keep him waiting, letting him see that he hadn't fooled me, that I wasn't scared of his craziness and his ugly face. Then I clasped his hand, the same hand, for the final throw.

This time I couldn't push him past the perpendicular. Our arms remained straight and trembling for what must have been a full minute. I made a mistake: I looked at his bruised face, the blackened eye, the swollen lip, the bruised cheekbone. His blue eyes bored into me, and I felt my arm weaken. I closed my eyes and concentrated on my exhausted muscles, ignoring the pain, willing my blood and sinews strength and success.

I imagined I was Rocky Sullivan. I had to win this match with the mob's most evil fighter, Edward G. Robinson. I hated him beyond reason. If I lost, then my girl was dead; they would kill her. If I won, they would set her free, and then we'd change our names and flee to South America where the mob could never find us.

I pushed with everything I had.

But it wasn't enough. With a cry, Bleeker found some raw unused power from somewhere deep inside himself and forced my trembling hand down on the tabletop. "Yaaaah!" he cried.

I could hear the ship's bell ring outside on the windy deck.

"Let's eat," said Bleeker, cheerful, friendlier than I'd ever seen him. "I'm starved."

TEN

The bathroom was brilliant. Everything dazzling white. Smashing.

With electric light. And posh, glossy white bogs in cubicles, with real toilet paper on little rollers set into the walls. And showers instead of bathtubs, three in each bathroom. And piles of thick white towels and facecloths on shelves; all you had to do was help yourself. I'd never taken a shower before. Today was only Thursday; I wasn't due for a bath, but I couldn't wait to try the shower. I'd seen them in movies and they looked like a lot of fun.

First I tried out the bogs. The seat had a hinged cover on it, real posh. Then I stripped and hopped into the shower. It took a while to figure out the controls. At first it was too cold, then it was too hot. I felt like Goldilocks. The soap was in a white wrapper that said "Ellerman's City Line" in blue. I tore it off. The clean scented smell reminded me of Beryl. I closed my eyes, thinking about her, and soaped myself all over, then stood under the waterfall, letting the hot water pound away on the back of my neck and shoulders. It was brilliant, phenomenal. Powerful, my dad would say.

I could have a shower every day if I wanted. Twice on Sundays and holy days. I laughed.

When I finally turned off the water, the bathroom was full of steam and I could hardly see my johnny wobbler. I wrapped myself in one of the thick white towels and stepped across the corridor back into our cabin. Bleeker was lying in his bunk picking his nose. His life jacket lay on the floor.

"You're supposed to keep this on," I said, throwing it up at him. "Go take a shower."

"Don't need one."

"You'll love it, Bleeker!"

"Had a bath last Sunday. Got three more days to go."

"Suit yourself."

I had to get away from Bleeker sharpish. I couldn't see how I was going to put up with him for ten days. I dressed, and traipsed about the ship and ended up in the playroom, where a bunch of noisy, snot-nosed kids were arguing over a board game. I grabbed a handful of old comics from a shelf and climbed up to the boat deck. Bright sunshine, a light breeze.

There was nobody else on this part of the deck. I found a spot behind a bulkhead out of the wind and sat on the deck with my phizog buried in the comics, trying to read, but thinking of Bleeker and having to put up with him for ten days. And then what? Canada. Far from home. I couldn't just run away, dragging myself through hedges of thorns, and sleeping in ditches. Where would I live in Canada? With strangers in a strange land.

The future lay on me like a weight.

It was quiet, just the sounds of the waves slopping against the sides of the ship. I looked up. Liverpool's spires and towers in the distance. Somewhere over there my mam and dad were getting on with their lives.

Without me.

"Pass the butter," said Bleeker.

"Please," said the boy opposite.

"Pass the butter, or I'll hammer yer stupid head on the table."

The boy sneered. "You couldn't hammer a penny nail." He almost threw the butter at Bleeker.

Bleeker was hoarding. There was nothing to put the butter on yet. We had only just sat down, eight to a table, and I could see no bread.

"Pass the water," said Bleeker.

A girl passed the water jug over. Bleeker filled his glass and drank.

There were about a hundred kids, and ten adult escorts like Miss Fisher, except the other escorts were older and not as pretty. The escorts were the only adult passengers sitting in the dining room; all the other adults on the ship, including the officers, I discovered later, ate at a different time.

Fish 'n' Chips's gang took up two tables, and appeared to range in age from about five or six—Elsie Bleeker—

to sixteen—the boy Bleeker had threatened over the butter, whose name, I found out later, was Tony Curtin. In my mind, I divided them into two groups: small kids, up to about ten years of age; and big ones, over ten. I counted eight small ones, girls mostly, and seven big ones, including myself and Bleeker.

I had tried to sit at the table away from Bleeker, but he'd followed and sat down beside me. I saw the others weigh up his snotty, oversized jacket. Then they looked at me and I glared back at them, trying to look tough like Bleeker.

Miss Fisher sat at our table. She took off her life jacket and pushed it under the table near her feet. The rest of us did the same. Bleeker's whiny little sister and her cabin partner, Patricia Richers, were busy arranging a life jacket on Elsie's chair so Elsie could reach the table comfortably. "There, try that," said Patricia.

Elsie climbed up onto the chair and sat down.

"That better?" said Patricia.

Elsie nodded and started to play with the silverware in front of her.

Each place had a blue linen napkin the same color as the tablecloth, and enough cutlery to start a shop. Like Buckingham Palace it was.

The waiters began with soup and bread. Bleeker quickly buttered several pieces of bread, and then began spooning his soup down before the rest of us all had ours. Miss Fisher, in her nice glossy voice, said, "We can begin our soup when everyone is served." But Bleeker took no

100

notice of her. By the time we all had soup, Bleeker had abandoned the spoon and was lifting his plate to his lips. He noisily finished the dregs with a quick backward tilt of his head and then wiped his plate clean with the bread. He was hungry.

Miss Fisher pretended not to notice. Tony Curtin watched Bleeker, a sneer on his lips.

Then there was white fish, fancy with white sauce and little bits of green stuff sprinkled on top. Unsure of what to do with all the knives and forks, I glanced about me to see what others were doing. But the other kids seemed just as baffled. We copied Miss Fisher. I could see the kids at the other table out of the corner of my eye; they were watching Fish 'n' Chips, too.

"Not much of a dinner, then," said Bleeker. "A skinny bit of old fish."

Miss Fisher smiled.

Patricia said, "That was only the second course." She laughed. "Ooh! I'll be as fat as an 'ippo by the time we get to Canada if I don't watch m'self!" She laughed again.

I watched the waiters, all Indian men with dark polished skin, looking absolutely brilliant in their white and pale blue uniforms with blue sashes about their waists, flitting quickly and silently about the huge room like fantastic, rare butterflies. My eyes were everywhere; they missed nothing. I had never eaten in a restaurant or a public dining room in my life. If only my mam and dad could see me now, I thought, and Charlie and the gang.

Next there was chicken—that's what Miss Fisher said

it was. I'd never had chicken before, only goose or turkey at Christmas in Ireland. It smelled good. It was done in a brown gravy, and there were two small potatoes with tiny bits of the same green stuff that was on the fish sitting on the tops; a small heap of green beans; a reddish thing, not turnip, for I knew what turnip was, but something like turnip, and three small mushrooms with a bit of green grassy stuff like carrot leaves on the top. The mushrooms were small and white with gray gills, not like the dark, brown-gilled velvety whoppers my grandad gathered for us to eat in Ireland.

Nobody talked much: we were all too busy trying to figure out which knife, which fork, how did you eat this, or what did you do with that.

But Bleeker didn't seem bothered by anything. Pigging his way through everything put in front of him, he used whichever knife or fork was handy, or used his fingers, licking them clean as he went along or wiping them on his snotty jacket. Then he mopped up the gravy on his messy plate with a fistful of bread. I looked at the others around the table; except for Tony Curtin, who was acting like a twerp, sneering at Bleeker over the top of the water jug, they didn't seem to be bothered by Bleeker's table manners.

Patricia helped Elsie use her knives and forks and napkin, sometimes stopping to wipe Elsie's chin or fingers.

I ate everything except the mushrooms. They looked nice, but what if they were poisonous ones? Better to be on the safe side: I left them on the side of the plate.

Dessert was pears with ice cream, and an extra big

bowl of ice cream left on the table in case anyone wanted more, which they did.

I thought we'd finished, but then the waiters, or stewards, as Miss Fisher called them, brought trays loaded with breads and crackers and many different kinds of cheese. Bleeker sampled all the cheeses, then cut pieces, several of each kind, and wrapped them in his napkin, which he pushed into his jacket pocket. Then came bowls of fruit: apples and oranges, plums and bananas.

Our eyes bugged out. Everyone reached for a banana or an orange; we hadn't seen either in a year. Some of the little kids didn't know what they were.

It was the best grub I'd ever had in my whole life.

We staggered away from the table.

Bleeker's big droopy jacket bulged all over.

The bunk, narrow but comfortable, wasn't too different from the one my dad made for me under the stairs. I lay wondering what they were doing right now. Probably thought I was well on my way to Canada; instead I was lying in a bunk with all my clothes on only a few miles from them, on a ship anchored in the middle of the Mersey. Was the house empty without me the way Madeleine said theirs was without Bren and Pat? Were they suffering the way the O'Doughertys were suffering? I hoped so. Traitors. I hoped they were sorry; I hoped they were crying buckets. I took out my new wallet and looked at the ten-bob note. Maybe they would change their minds and send a boat out to bring me back. I untied the green silk rope from around my middle and dropped it on the floor beside my shoes. Maybe there was a boat on the way to fetch me this very minute. I listened.

Silence. Except for the low creak of boards and ropes, and an occasional groan from the anchor chain.

I could smell Bleeker's rotten socks and underwear on the floor where he'd dropped them.

I was in a foul mood. I'd eaten too much; a cannonball weighted my stomach. I kicked the bunk above my head.

"Cut it out," Bleeker growled.

He was still awake. I kicked his bunk again so he'd think I wasn't scared of him.

"Cut it out!" Louder.

"You're supposed to wear your clothes to bed."

Silence.

"The least you could do is put your smelly socks and underwear in the bag in the wardrobe."

"I did."

"No you didn't. It's not the smell so much that bothers me, it's the way it makes my eyes smart."

"Very funny."

"I wasn't being funny. Me—*my*," I corrected myself, "my eyes are watering with the stink."

"Sod off."

I kicked his bunk again.

"I said cut it out!"

"Not until you put your smelly things in the bag."

I heard him move and start to climb down. I thought

he was coming to pound me. I swung my feet onto the floor, ready, just in case.

But I needn't have worried. He threw his stuff into the laundry bag, closed the wardrobe door, and climbed back to bed. I was surprised. Maybe the smell was getting to him, too.

"You should go take a shower, Bleeker."

Silence.

"You'd never regret it."

"Shurrup or I'll flatten your phizog for ye."

The ship wasn't moving much, hardly at all, just enough to rock me to sleep.

I thought I heard sirens in the night, but I slept on. Nobody came to wake me up.

Breakfast was not quite so many knives and forks. There was grapefruit—real, not in a tin; cornflakes; as much milk as you liked; real eggs, not that yellow powder they called dried eggs; and as much bacon as you wanted.

I couldn't understand why no ration books were needed on the *Benares*, why there was so much food, when my mam always had to search and queue for every scrap. "I got a lovely bit of fresh skate at Malone's, Nan," Mrs. Costello would shout up the yard to my mam. Or a nice bit of pork dripping at the butcher's, or whatever, and my mam would throw on her coat, grab her shopping bag, and hurry down Precky Road to join the queue. Sometimes, by the time she got there, it was all gone.

Elsie Bleeker seemed happier, no whining, making

friends with a couple of little kids in our group. She still carried Dolly everywhere she went.

"After breakfast there will be medicals for you and your sister," Miss Fisher said to Bleeker. "And you too, Jamie. The three of you came late and missed medicals ashore."

Bleeker scowled. "I don't need no medical."

"Rules," said Miss Fisher with a smile. "They won't let you into Canada unless you're healthy."

"That'll be fine with me," I said.

Dr. Watterson's office was on the promenade deck. Elsie went in first, clutching her doll as usual. She was in a long time. When she came out, she was carrying a small paper bag. She sat down and Bleeker went in.

"I gotta clean my teeth," said Elsie proudly. "Every morning and every night 'fore I go to bed. The doctor give me my own toothbrush 'n' toothpaste." She opened her paper bag and held it out for me to look.

Bleeker's scowl was tighter than usual when he came out. He was trying to hide his paper bag in his fist. He said to his sister, "Let's go, worm! Move yer legs!"

I went in.

Dr. Watterson was a nice old geezer. "Take off your things," he said.

I took off my life jacket, my shoes and socks, and then my blazer, jersey, vest, and my navy blue trousers, until all I had left on was my cotton underpants.

When he was finished prodding and tapping and weighing me, and searching in my hair for nits and lice, he said, "Put your things back on again, Jamie." Then he said, "Take this brush and show me how you brush your teeth." He gave me a new brush, blue.

I showed him.

"Good. What about toothpaste?"

"Thanks, but I've got lots."

"You're a fine healthy boy, Jamie," said the doctor as he scribbled in his book.

I meandered back to the cabin. Bleeker was lying in his bunk, picking his nose and recovering from his medical examination. There came a knock on the door. Bleeker jumped down off his bunk to open it.

A man stood there, an Indian with brown eyes like soup bowls and a cheerful grin. He wore a white jacket and was carrying a bulging bag over his shoulder.

"What do ye want?" said Bleeker roughly.

"Dirty laundry," said the man.

Bleeker stepped back and let him in. The man took the bag from the bottom of the wardrobe and left an empty one in its place. Then he pinned a metal tag to our laundry bag and tossed it into his big carryall. "Tank-you-very-much," he said, making it sound like all one word.

An alarm went off. Bells clanged. I said, "What is it?"

"Boat drill," said the man, grinning.

We hurried up to the playroom on the promenade deck. Miss Fisher was already there, inspecting life jackets and counting the fifteen heads.

"Follow me," said Fish 'n' Chips. We marched out to the starboard side of the promenade deck and stood about like a bunch of idiots—eejits, as the Irish say—waiting, while above us on the boat deck an officer and several Indian deck hands were busy mucking about with the ropes, making our lifeboat ready for launching. Twenty or so Indians, one of them our cabin steward, stood with us in rows like they were in the army. I was expecting Miss Fisher to tell us to get in rows, too, but she didn't.

Our lifeboat was lowered. The tall thin officer with the beard, the one who had told us about the mines, called for attention. Then he said, "I am Third Officer Seeley and I will be in charge of this lifeboat. If you have questions, please ask them now."

Silence.

"Begin boarding the lifeboat," said Seeley. "Children first."

Me and the Bleekers and Patricia Richers were the last of our lot to climb in the boat. Next was Miss Fisher, and a bunch of adult passengers we hadn't seen before because they kept themselves separate in the front of the ship. The Indian crew climbed in last, and we all sat in the boat in our bulky life jackets like peas in a pod, watching the people in one of the other lifeboats ahead of us, and craning our necks to see the crew handling the ropes up on the boat deck over our heads.

The weather was fine, with a slight breeze coming at us from the blue-green distance that was the mouth of the river. We all had full bellies. Except for the older adult passengers, a bunch of nervous ninnies, everyone seemed to be enjoying the drill.

There was a mast lying along the center of the lifeboat

on a hinge meant to raise it from horizontal to vertical. I could see several built-in, wooden storage lockers along the starboard side. On the opposite, port, side, two pairs of oars were secured to the inside of the boat with leather strapping. What seemed to interest Bleeker most, however, was ten winding handles attached to the gunwales, five on each side of the boat. Bleeker sat and wound one of the handles like he was winding a gramophone, and I could see an oiled gear wheel turning underneath the gunwale. The gearwheel was connected to a shaft in the bottom of the boat. I leaned over the back of the boat and saw that Bleeker's efforts were causing a big brass propeller to turn very slowly underneath the rudder. The work was hard, and Bleeker soon gave up.

The boy sitting next to me was a blabber. He usually sat at our table with Tony Curtin. His name was Rob Grice, from London, and he was fourteen. A bit on the heavy side, he was, plump as a butcher's dog. What my mam would call a big lump. He wore glasses. He was telling me that his house had got a direct hit. Luckily, he was in their Anderson shelter at the time with his mam and dad.

"I seen lots of dead ones," he said.

"Corpses?" I said.

He nodded. "Like you wouldn't believe."

I looked across at Bleeker. He was listening attentively to Grice.

"I seen 'em pick up body parts from bomb sites," said Grice, "and try to fit 'em together, an arm 'ere, a leg there, sometimes an 'ead—"

I didn't want to hear any more. I said, "I wonder how long this boat drill will take?" But Grice blabbed on. I closed my ears.

Bleeker opened one of the lockers: blankets. He opened another: tins of food. He reached in and pulled out a big bar of chocolate, which he dropped into his jacket pocket.

Third Officer Seeley and another officer checked the launching ropes, then inspected us all, making sure our life jackets were tied properly; and the drill was over. We climbed out of the lifeboat and the crew hauled it back up to the boat deck again.

There were deck games, quoits, hopscotch, stuff like that, but Bleeker didn't join in. He went off to our cabin. I stayed and watched the games for a while. Elsie sat her doll down on the deck and played hopscotch with her two friends while Patricia watched over them like an old mother hen. I strolled down and had another shower, the second in two days! I'd never been so clean in my whole life: it felt good. Maybe the ship wouldn't ever move out of the river; we'd all stay here for the rest of the war, eating bananas and oranges and ice cream and playing games and having lifeboat drills and hot showers. And my mam and dad would think I was in Canada. I wouldn't tell them I was still here, only a few miles away from them, bobbing about in the estuary like a cork.

After my shower, I tried to ditch Bleeker in the cabin and go off on my own with an old *Adventure* comic, one I'd read before, but he followed me.

"You don't have to come with me, Bleeker," I said.

"I'm just going for a wander around the ship. Why don't you stay and relax and stuff your face with the emergency rations you stole from the lifeboat."

Sarcasm was lost on him. "I don't mind," he said, like he was doing me a favor.

We went all over the ship. He offered me some of his chocolate, but I gave him a look and he put it back in his pocket. We had nothing to say to each other.

We leaned over the ship's side looking down at the muddy brown water. Bleeker reached into his jacket pocket, pulled out a handful of dinner table crackers, and started throwing them at the screeching sea gulls, trying to hit them, giving a yell of satisfaction whenever he succeeded.

The *Benares* upped anchor and sailed at six o'clock. It was Friday the thirteenth. The weather closed in and brought wind and rain. We headed for the open sea. I stood with Bleeker on the deck, shivering with the cold, thinking about my mam and dad and looking back at Liverpool as it disappeared behind us in the rain and gloom.

ELEVEN

I was ill.

I had never felt so deadly sick in my whole life.

It was Saturday morning.

It had started last night as soon as the ship hit the open sea. The wind and rain had increased, and we'd rolled and pitched, and my stomach, full of its second dinner— roast pork this time—had been the first to rebel. I ran to the side and threw up. I wanted to die.

Then I collapsed on my bunk.

"Your face is green," said Bleeker, grinning. He hadn't been affected by the awful roll and pitch of the ship.

"Go and ask Fish 'n' Chips to come and see me," I gasped.

"Go yourself."

"I'm sick, dammit! I think I'm dying!"

Eventually, after I'd moaned and groaned, and Bleeker could stand it no longer, he went. He was back in under a minute. "She can't come. She's sick herself. She said to drink some water and keep warm in bed."

"You didn't go!" I accused him.

"I did so. She's sick. Almost everyone's sick. The pork must have been off."

"It's not the pork, you idiot. It's the ship!"

"Then how come I feel all right?"

"Because you're not human, Bleeker. You're a flaming freak!"

"If you weren't so green and ugly, I'd punch you on the nose."

I don't know how I got through the night. I kept dozing and waking, and running and dry-heaving over the side of the ship like some old geezer outside the Black Horse pub on Precky Road hawking up a gob of yellow snot.

In the morning, the nurse came to the cabin and gave me some foul-tasting stuff that must have come from the bilge. Her name tag said "Nurse Joan Appleton." "All the passengers are sick," she said cheerfully. "But you'll be fine tomorrow, once you have your sea legs."

When she'd gone, Bleeker offered me some of his stolen cheese, holding out a smelly, weeping green lump that looked like it was full of maggots. "Have some, Monaghan." He leered. "It'll settle yer stomach."

I rushed out to the deck and hung over the rail, retching. The *Benares* was a coal-burner; the smell from the funnels made me gag even more.

After that, the cabin steward came. He knocked on the door, and when there was no answer, he came in and saw

113

me lying in the bunk. He grinned, dark eyes sparkling. "Very-sick?"

I groaned.

He dropped the laundry bag on the floor, reached into his tunic pocket, took out a small brown paper bag, and emptied a few dark seeds from the bag onto the palm of my hand. "Chew-this, very-good-stuff. Make you-feel-bit-better."

I looked. "What is it?"

"Fennel. Very-good."

I chewed. It tasted like cow shit. "Thanks."

He grinned happily. "You are veree-welcome."

"You're from India."

He nodded his head vigorously. "From-Bombay. I am-Karam."

"Karam?"

"That-is-right. Karam."

"I'm Jamie. I'm thirteen." I saw no harm in adding the extra weeks. The fennel seemed to be working a bit. Or maybe it was Karam's cheerful phizog.

"I-go-Jamee. Much-work."

Karam's medicine worked for only a short time. Then I felt bad again. I avoided the dining room. But Bleeker didn't. In the afternoon I staggered out onto the deck. It was deserted. I leaned over the side, trying to be sick, but there was nothing there. It felt like my stomach was trying to throw up my brains.

I looked at the seascape through watery eyes. Gray. Everything was gray, sea and sky were all one, lifeless and drab. The ship was in the middle of nowhere, rolling and pitching to the end of the world.

The bells clanged.

Oh no! I couldn't believe it, a fire drill! I'd have to skip out; I couldn't possibly make it up to the muster station. I staggered back to the cabin. Bleeker had been looking for me.

"Boat drill." He grinned, and grabbed my arm and began dragging me along the deck while I spluttered and moaned for him to leave me be.

Miss Fisher looked terrible. So did just about everyone else. She gathered us all together and led the way to the boat station, where we stood swaying and groaning, hanging on to the nearest solid piece of the landscape.

This time we didn't have to climb into the boat. The crew on the boat deck lowered the boat only partway, and then we were inspected and dismissed by Mr. Seeley and the deck officer.

I clawed my way back to my bunk and stayed there for the rest of the day and the night, only dimly aware of Bleeker's comings and goings.

It seemed to me at one time that Bleeker shook me, trying to wake me, yelling something about a submarine, and I told him to sod off, but that was probably a dream.

I crawled gingerly from my bunk Sunday morning. Bleeker was out, gone to breakfast, I guessed. I went out on deck. The ship was rolling slowly, gracefully nosing through a choppy, sparkling green sea. There was pale sunshine. The air smelled clean, newly washed in the pearly light of morning. I felt better. Not hungry, but definitely better.

I took a shower. The place was full of steam. I could hear someone in the next cubicle. I stood under the hot spray, letting the water batter my skin. Then I soaped myself all over and stood again under the spray. It felt good.

I stepped out of the shower and grabbed for a towel off the rack. And saw Bleeker standing there naked, his johnny wobbler sticking out like an extra thumb. He was peering into the steamed-up mirror.

When he realized I was there, he snatched a towel to cover his shoulders and turned his back to me, but I had already seen the dark welts on his white arms, shoulders, and back.

Pretending I'd seen nothing, I whisked a towel off the shelf. "Your bath day, is it, Bleeker?"

"You must be feeling better," said Bleeker without turning around. "That toffee-nosed Scouse sneer is back in your voice."

"How did you like the shower?"

"You and that sneery English twerp with the la-di-da accent would make the great pals." He meant Tony Curtin.

"Ever had a shower before?"

No reply.

"I expect everyone in Belfast had showers, eh?" I wanted to get on his wick, wanted to needle him, I didn't know why.

Silence.

"Did you take a bath every week, or only if you really needed one?"

Bleeker turned and looked at me. "I saw a submarine."

"Huh?"

"A German U-boat. I saw one."

"Where?"

"He was sitting on the surface like a fly on a pool of piss. I saw him. Far, far away on the horizon he was. But it was a U-boat all right."

"It was probably a reflection on the—"

"I saw him, I'm telling you! I got eyes like a shitehawk, my da says so. It was a U-boat."

It was the first time Bleeker had ever mentioned his dad. "If it was really a U-boat, you would've told someone."

"I did. I told one of them fancy uniform jackeens."

"An officer. What did he say?"

"He looked through his binoculars, but couldn't see nothing, gormless galoot—the U-boat had gone by then. Asked me what it looked like and I told him, but he still didn't believe me."

"So what did you do?"

"I tried to get in and see the captain, but they wouldn't let me. Asked me why I wanted to see him and I told them, but they didn't believe me neither. Said if there was a U-boat, then the navy destroyer would know about it because they can hear them miles away."

"It might have been one of the ships in our convoy. They're all spread out over several miles, you know."

117

"We're being followed, I know that much. He's underneath us, like a bloody shark, waiting to strike."

I didn't know what to think. Bleeker was still worried about sailing on Friday the thirteenth, if you ask me. His fears and imagination were making him see submarines.

"You don't believe me either, do you?"

"I didn't say that."

"Ye don't need to. I can see it in yer face. Are ye going to mass?"

"Is there a mass?"

"Better be quick. Prom deck, ten o'clock." Bleeker headed for the cabin, one towel knotted about his skinny waist, and another hanging about his neck and shoulders.

I shouldn't have been surprised there was a mass. As well as a doctor and a nurse, there were also two ministers on the ship, one Church of England, the Reverend Goss, and the other Catholic, Father Rigby. Not the same Rigby as the one at Snozzy's, of course. Funny that, two Rigbys. Maybe all the Irish Rigby families had a rule that boys become priests. Snozzy's Father Rigby wrote a hymn specially for Snozzy's church:

> Hail St. Oswald, we salute thee,
> Our great Patron, Martyr, King;
> In this church which bears thy title,
> Joyously thy praise we sing.

We used to sing it in church and at school all the time, and often when me and Bren and Charlie and Gordie were traipsing through Chilly Woods looking for horse chestnuts or birds' eggs on a Saturday, we'd sing it because of its fine marching rhythm.

What I was surprised about was Bleeker wanting to go to mass. I would have thought he'd be just the kind to skip out if nobody was watching.

Did I want to go to mass? It was a mortal sin if you skipped Sunday mass. I often thought of skipping. But if I died in a state of mortal sin, I'd go straight to hell. I could never figure out why. Just for missing mass you spend the rest of eternity in the all-consuming flames. Didn't make sense to me. Best to be on the safe side, though.

By the time I'd rubbed myself dry with one of the Ellerman's City Line towels, I felt like my old self again.

There was no singing, only Father Rigby's droning voice, most of the words lost in the fresh wind.

It was good to feel well again.

Red canvas folding chairs, with missals on the seats, had been laid out neatly across the deck. Most of the seats were empty. I sat in the row behind Bleeker and it made me think of the last time I'd sat behind him; he had been drawing a Spitfire instead of dahlias as Beryl Oyler made cow eyes at him. That was only a few days ago; it seemed like a century.

I thought about the marks on his back and shoulders. Cruel bruises. His thin body was black and blue with them. Too many and in the wrong places to have been caused by Stinky Corcoran. Besides, except for the one in the stomach, Stinky's blows had all been to the head. Someone had been beating Bleeker, that much was obvious. His mam'd had bruises, too. So it must be the dad. Those nights when he came in drunk. Maybe that was how Bleeker got his black eye, the one he'd had when he started at Snozzy's. Possibly Elsie also had hidden bruises, though I didn't think so somehow.

Bleeker had his head bent over his missal, following the mass. Not like me, letting my thoughts wander wherever they led, all over the place like a drunk pissing up against a wall. My mind was always a free rover during mass because it was so boring with everyone muttering in Latin and bending and bobbing and bowing all the time. I'd tried sneaking a comic into the missal one time, but it was too awkward, and my mam almost turned herself inside out she was so furious.

I thought about the German U-boat. Had Bleeker really seen one? I moved my eyes away from Bleeker's earnest profile and his jacket like a tent around his shoulders, and scanned the horizon. Nothing. I turned my head and looked behind. Only an old freighter, much too far away to read the name on its bow.

I gradually became aware of people singing on the lower deck. Goss's bunch of Proddies. I listened. "Eternal Father, strong to save," came the Protestant voices, reminding me of the billboard, the one down by the Old Swan Library with the old man in the nice suit, reaching out toward you. PLACE YOURSELF IN OUR HANDS.

Without music, our service was a desert with no water. Not for Bleeker, though. He seemed lost in his missal and the mass, standing and genuflecting, up and down like a fiddler's elbow, and making signs of the cross in all the right places without having to look around at what everyone else was doing the way I had to if my mam was watching me.

Right after mass there was another boat drill. We had to climb into the boat. This time Officer Seeley climbed in with us and sat up in the bow looking down on us all, and ordering the crew about so that ten of them ended up sitting beside the mechanical hand levers on the sides of the lifeboat. I tried to avoid Grice, but he sat opposite, and started telling a funny story about his Uncle Rory, who was Irish.

"Uncle Rory listened to Lord 'Aw-'Aw on the wireless every night. Believed everything 'e said, too."

"Who's Lord Haw-Haw?" said Bleeker.

Tony Curtin, the sixteen-year-old, sneered, "Don't you know *anything*, Irish? Haw-Haw's British, a traitor, went over to the German side, and broadcasts on the radio from Germany."

"Don't call me Irish," said Bleeker.

"Why not? That's where you're from, isn't it? Ireland, the neutral country?"

Bleeker glared at him. "Northern Ireland is in the war, helping the English."

"Lord 'Aw-'Aw," said Grice quickly, "is trying to get England to surrender by scaring the crap out of them. My Uncle Rory wanted the Germans to win the war because 'Itler promised Ireland that once 'e'd beaten England 'e'd give them their own country back, you see. So

Uncle Rory didn't even put up 'is Anderson, didn't think 'e needed it, didn't think the Jerries would ever drop a bomb on 'im, y'see, being on their side an' all. Not too bright, my Uncle Rory. Anyway, a Junkers dropped a bomb in the next street. Blew Uncle Rory right out the winder, it did. Ended up in the street under a milk van. Lucky 'e wasn't killed, silly old fool. Eh eh eh." Grice laughed. " 'E was like a bee in a jar. Swore at 'Itler, and at 'Aw-'Aw next time 'e come on. Next day my Uncle Rory was out in 'is yard diggin' a shelter. Eh eh eh." He laughed again.

Elsie cuddled her doll and sat up front with Patricia. I could hear Patricia's voice and her laugh, as she enjoyed playing the mother to Bleeker's sister, while chattering at the same time to Laura and Theresa about a movie called *Gone With the Wind,* which she'd seen three times. "Wasn't Scarlett O'Hara divine?" she was asking them.

The only O'Hara I knew was the teacher at Snozzy's, and she wasn't exactly divine.

Bleeker helped himself to another bar of chocolate from the emergency rations.

Curtin saw him. "Put that back, Bleeker, or I'll tell the lifeboat officer."

"Go ahead and tell," said Bleeker.

"It's emergency food," said Curtin. "What if we had to use this lifeboat and you've already eaten all the rations? Perfectly beastly behavior I call it."

"Sod off!"

122

Curtin glared contemptuously at Bleeker, but said no more.

Tony Curtin had a posh English accent like Miss Fisher's. He had a narrow face, long nose, and fine fair hair that fell in a careless clump over his right eye. I didn't much like him; he acted kind of superior, but if you ask me, I think he was right to tell Bleeker off about the chocolate.

Later, after the drill, Bleeker went down to the cabin. To avoid him, I climbed up to the boat deck and leaned on the rail with Curtin watching the green ocean foam against the ship's flanks, like looking into a flushing toilet. Though the boat deck was high above the engine room I could feel the vibration of the ship's engines. In the distance I could make out the dark shapes of other ships in the convoy. The *Benares* led the others, but slowly. We seemed to be limping along like an old broken-down Wallasey ferryboat across the Mersey.

"We're not going very fast," I said.

"Only half speed," said Curtin. "It's because we can only go as fast as the slowest ship in the convoy. So the others can keep up."

"How do you know?"

"Dunne told me."

"Who's Dunne?"

"The fourth officer, the one trying to grow a mustache."

"Isn't that more dangerous?" I said.

"Growing a mustache?" Curtin sniggered.

"No. I mean only going half speed."

"Yes, it's dangerous," said Curtin, "but with a destroyer and two sloops escorting us, Jerry wouldn't dare. Look! There's the destroyer now!" He pointed. Gray, sleek, and deadly, bristling with guns, it cut through the convoy like a greyhound.

We continued leaning on the rail after it had gone, looking out at the sea and the other shadowy ship shapes off in the distance, saying nothing for a while. I wondered whether to tell Curtin about Bleeker's U-boat, but decided not to.

"Were you seasick?" said Curtin.

"Awful."

"Me too. Thought I was dying. Still a bit wobbly actually. Didn't seem to affect your friend, though."

"Bleeker? He's not me—my friend. We just happen to be sharing the same cabin."

"I don't like him; he's a rotter. Common as dirt."

I didn't know why, but I felt a sudden flush of guilt.

"No he's not," I hurried to say. "He—he's all right, Bleeker, just a bit rough, that's all. But he's all right."

"Eats like a pig. Can't stand him. That's his sister, isn't it? The little one with the . . ." He flicked a finger at his hair.

"Bleeker's all right."

"What happened to his face, a fight?"

"Yes."

"I'm not a bit surprised somebody beat him up. He'll be getting a few straight lefts from me before very long if he doesn't watch his dirty mouth."

I said nothing.

Curtin was quiet for a while. Then he said, "Did you want to come away, Monaghan? To leave home, I mean?"

"No."

"Neither did I actually. But so many people were being killed in London."

"I know."

"I feel a bit happier about it now, being sent away," said Curtin. "I'm rather beginning to enjoy myself. Like an adventure, if you know what I mean."

I looked at him. He was three years older than me. I wished I could see the whole thing as an adventure. But I couldn't lie to myself: the only place I really wanted to be was home in 19 Baden Road with my mam and dad.

TWELVE

"Most of the kids around our way played with bricks from the bombed 'ouses," said Patricia Richers, "making—"

"Pass the butter," said Bleeker to Curtin.

"Please!" demanded Laura and Theresa together.

"Get it yourself, Irish," said Curtin.

Bleeker said nothing. He seemed out of it. Something on his mind. Still thinking about his sub if you ask me.

Laura passed the butter, but not without rolling her eyes at Theresa.

Curtin caught Grice's eye, and his lips parted in the beginning of a sneer.

Lunchtime, Sunday. Our gang seemed to have sorted itself out so that we were all starting to sit in the same seats. The big kids—me and Bleeker, Curtin, Grice, Laura, Theresa, Patricia—and little Elsie sat at one table; the small kids sat with Miss Fisher at the second table.

All we seemed to do on the ship was eat.

But our appetites had leveled out, become accustomed to the abundance of good grub, and we'd stopped stuffing ourselves like starving gannets. Even Bleeker took his time, didn't grab at everything, didn't pack his pockets with crackers and cheese, though Laura and Theresa, probably influenced by Curtin's good looks and perfect manners, had started to make fun of Bleeker's different ways.

"Don't you know it's bad manners to eat with your elbows on the table?" said Theresa, the thin dark one with glasses.

"And you're s'posed to shut your mouth when you're eating," said Laura, plump and blond.

"Shut your gobs," said Bleeker calmly.

"Bricks from the bomb sites," Patricia repeated, ignoring Theresa and Laura's glares at Bleeker. "They all 'ad a fine old time building little 'ouses for themselves to play in. Used doors for the roof, they did. You'd be surprised 'ow good some of them was, proper little bricklayers. Ha!"

Patricia's warmth and good-natured chatter were the only cement that held our table together.

"I know," Grice said across the table to Patricia. "The kids in my street did the same thing. They 'ad another game, too, piling bricks to see who could build the 'ighest tower wivout it toppling down."

Curtin wasn't eating but was staring sourly at Bleeker, who was licking Dover sole and butter off his fingers, his elbows on the table.

"Someone should teach you how to use a knife and—" Theresa started to say to Bleeker, but I cut her off.

127

"Knives and forks don't matter," I said, putting down my knife and fork and picking up a piece of fish from my plate with my fingers. I was getting fed up with them all picking on him. Bleeker was no friend of mine, but we were both Irish, after all. "What matters is that we're here and we're alive instead of lying dead under a pile of bricks." I licked the sauce off my fingers the way I'd seen Bleeker do it.

Bleeker stared at me.

"You're right, Monaghan," said Grice with a grin. "We're lucky to be out of it."

Patricia leaned over the table toward Curtin. "You're quiet today, Tony. And you're not eating much. Are you all right?"

"I'm perfectly well, actually," said Curtin. He pushed back his chair and tossed his napkin onto the table. "But Bleeker makes me feel sick."

"You'll feel sick all right if I bash your stupid head in," said Bleeker, scowling.

"I would like to see you try it," sneered Curtin.

Bleeker glared at him.

Curtin got up and left the dining room.

"Ooh! What's the matter wiv 'im, then?" said Patricia.

"Can I have some more milk?" said Elsie.

I hadn't seen Bleeker since lunch. He wasn't in the cabin. I wondered idly where he'd got to. Good riddance, I thought. But when he still hadn't shown up an hour before dinner, I set off to look for him.

I found him up on the boat deck behind a lifeboat,

sheltering from the wind. He was staring out to sea through a pair of binoculars.

"You're looking for that U-boat, aren't you, Bleeker?"

He didn't answer me.

"Where did you get the binoculars?"

"I borrowed them."

"Who from?"

No answer.

"What I don't understand," I said, "is why a U-boat would be on the surface. If it was really a U-boat, he'd be under the water, wouldn't he?"

"Not while he was hurrying to catch up with us he wouldn't. He's slow underwater. Travels faster on the surface."

"He does?"

"He stays beyond the horizon out of sight. Then at night, when nobody can see him, he moves in close and follows, waiting for the right time to strike."

"How do you know so much about U-boats?"

"Dunne told me."

Dunne was the officer Tony Curtin had mentioned, the one growing the mustache.

"Does he believe you saw one?"

Bleeker lowered the binoculars and looked up at me. "No. When there's a destroyer escort, a U-boat runs the other way as fast as it can. That's what he said."

"But you don't believe him."

"No."

"How do you expect to see the U-boat if he's under the water?"

"Periscope."

I didn't say anything, but if you ask me, the chances of seeing a periscope sticking up out of the water in this choppy sea were absolutely nil. Besides, it was getting dark, and I was starting to shiver with the cold. "Give up, Bleeker. It's almost dinnertime."

He didn't answer me. I left him there and headed for the shower.

At Monday's breakfast, Patricia was telling about when she'd been evacuated a year ago at the outbreak of the war and had been sent with her school pals to a town in the English Cotswolds.

"Chippin' Campden it was called," said Patricia, "and me and my friend Mavis was put wiv a nice old lady named Mrs. Church. Well, you'll laugh, I know, but she put us upstairs in this lovely room with a big bed, and when it come time to turn in, me and Mavis went to sleep on the floor, not realizing we was supposed to lie in the nice bed. Ooh! Mrs. Church was shocked when she seen us lying on the floor like we did at 'ome. The bed was for us, not 'er! She must've thought we was proper funny. Ha!"

"That's nothing," said Laura. "I was sent—"

"Sshhh!" said Theresa.

The room had fallen silent as the Reverend Goss stood to speak. He waited until everyone was quiet, and then he said, "I would like to make a few announcements. First, you will all be happy to know that we are now well out of the Atlantic U-boat danger zone."

Cheers.

Bleeker gave me a look.

"Since we are now safe from U-boats, you may, if you like, undress for bed each night. But keep your clothes handy just in case."

More cheers.

"I see that we have all recovered from our touch of sea-sickness."

Groans. A few cheers.

"Next, the news from England is most encouraging: yesterday the Royal Air Force shot down 185 German planes."

Loud cheers and whoops.

The Reverend Goss beamed with pleasure.

"Finally, the captain has asked me to tell you that, in celebration of the British victory, there will be a special tea party at lunchtime today, here in the dining room."

Ecstatic cheers and whoops.

Goss sat down, his face red and smiling.

At noon there were paper party hats to wear, crackers to pull, and ice cream and cake to eat. The room had been decorated with colored streamers. You'd think the war was over, the way they were all going on. Daft if you ask me.

Miss Fisher was wearing a green dress and stockings and had her hair pinned up. She looked smashing. Elsie and the other small kids, eight of them all together, sat at their own table laughing and giggling and spooning cake and ice cream into their phizogs. Miss Fisher had moved to the big kids' table, and sat between Theresa and Laura. Patricia and Curtin were listening to Rob Grice tell a story about his sister and her husband, who lived in Wimbledon. Bleeker, sitting beside Patricia, was busily eating.

Patricia turned to Bleeker. "You're Irish, right?"

Bleeker nodded without looking at her. "From Belfast."

"My mum come from Killarney," said Patricia, "years ago when she was a girl."

Bleeker said nothing.

"She took me there once when I was a kid to this big 'ouse with acres and acres of green, green grass, and the 'ouse 'ad h'old oil paintings and h'old furniture, and—"

I couldn't hear the rest. The room was noisier than Lime Street Station with two trains building a head of steam for London and Lancaster. A few of the escorts had organized their groups for a singsong. They started with "Roll Out the Barrel."

Curtin said to me over the noise, "Isn't that great about the RAF shooting down all those Germans, Monaghan? By the time we reach Canada, the war will be over." He pulled a face. "Just when we're starting to enjoy ourselves."

"Don't worry," I said. "My dad says the war won't be over for another six months."

"And we're out of the U-boat zone, that's good news, too," said Patricia, who had given up on Bleeker.

Bleeker said, "I don't see how they can be so sure."

"Oh, but they are sure," said Patricia. "We're in the

middle of the Atlantic. U-boats don't come this far, do they, Miss Fisher?" she said, raising her voice across the table.

Fish 'n' Chips leaned forward. "I can't hear . . ."

"U-boats don't come this far out, isn't that right?"

Miss Fisher opened her mouth to answer, but Grice chipped in. "That's right. We're safe. We don't really need the Royal Navy escort no more."

Miss Fisher got up to take care of a small kid who had started crying at the other table.

Curtin, sneery voice, said, "Bleeker thinks we're being followed by a U-boat, isn't that right, Bleeker?"

Bleeker looked at me. I shrugged, letting him know it wasn't me who'd told him.

"Are you scared, Bleeker?" said Curtin. "Afraid, are you? Trembling with fear, are you?" He pushed back his floppy hair and laughed. Grice and Laura and Theresa laughed, too. "That's why the Irish stayed out of the war," continued Curtin. "They're all too scared. Everyone knows the Irish are cowards."

Bleeker's face went white. "Take that back or I'll flatten ye!"

"You couldn't flatten a five-pound note," Curtin taunted. "You're nothing but a beastly coward!"

"Come outside and prove it," said Bleeker quietly.

"I don't strike children," said Curtin, "but sometimes a nasty child deserves a thrashing." He stood. "It will be a pleasure to teach you a few manners, Irish." He turned and led the way from the dining room. Bleeker got up and followed. I looked at Grice; he looked at me. As we hurried after them, I saw Laura and Theresa speaking urgently to Miss Fisher.

"Better go up to the boat deck," Grice advised Bleeker and Curtin when we got outside. "Fisher's coming."

We hurried up the stairs to a spot behind a ventilator. Curtin, older and taller, was smirking. Bleeker looked worried. They let their jackets fall to the deck. Curtin raised his fists and dropped his shoulder, professional-like, as though he'd had plenty of lessons in boxing. Bleeker, hands by his sides, just stared at him. Curtin advanced, dancing on his toes, fists circling. Bleeker stepped inside those long arms, grabbed Curtin by the shirt, and butted him in the face with his head.

Curtin fell to the deck, the old red stuff pouring out of his schnozz like paint from a can.

The fight was over in two seconds. I couldn't believe it. Bleeker picked up his jacket off the deck and walked away. Curtin, a fist clamped on his nose, yelled after him, "Dirty fighter! Dirty fighter!"

"That was a Belfast kiss," Bleeker shouted back over his shoulder. "Let me know when you need another one."

Me and Grice—Grice and I—helped Curtin up and sat him down by the ventilator ledge and told him to keep his head back to stop the bleeding.

After a while the bleeding stopped.

"What did I tell you," cried Curtin. "He's a beastly coward."

THIRTEEN

I tossed about in my bunk that night unable to sleep, listening to the throb of the ship's engines underneath me. I was still playing it safe, wearing my clothes and my life jacket in bed, in spite of old Goss's confident relaxation of the rules.

Bleeker was asleep; I could hear him muttering his way through his dreams, as he usually did. During the second night, which was the first one at sea, when I was sick, I woke once and thought I heard him crying out, but I couldn't be sure it wasn't myself.

But last night he had muttered in his sleep. And in the early hours his loud cries woke me.

My thoughts ran in circles, from my mam and dad, to Bleeker, to Bren and Gordie and Charlie, to Bleeker, to my burned room, to Canada, to gangster movies, back to Bleeker again.

Curtin had called it dirty fighting. I pondered. Dirty

fighting was punching below the belt, or using your elbows, or your knees or feet. I'd never heard of anyone using their head. I pondered some more. Butting a galoot in the phizog didn't seem quite fair, though. I reached a decision: that *was* dirty fighting, Curtin was right. But what a thrill! I'd never seen anyone do that before—what had Bleeker called it? A Belfast kiss? The excitement had fizzed up in me when Curtin went down with the bloody nose. Butted him in the face like a ram. Phew! He could've done that to Stinky Corcoran if he'd wanted. Why didn't he? Bleeker was a puzzle.

Maybe it was Curtin calling the Irish cowards.

My mam and dad were Irish, and so was I. What if someone said that to *me*—that the Irish were cowards? Would I have fought them? I didn't think so. That bothered me. I wasn't tough enough. Not like Bleeker. Maybe I was a coward.

Belfast kiss. Bleeker was a powerful fighter right enough.

It was hot in the cabin. I kicked off the blanket.

Madeleine. If anyone called the Irish cowards in front of red, fiery Madeleine, she'd brain them with a statue of St. Theresa. Ha!

Was my dad ever in a fight? I'd never thought to ask him.

My mam and dad.

We'd never been separated before. I hated them for sending me away.

But I missed them, too.

Dad was from the west of Ireland, from Mayo. Mam

was from the east, Kildare. I could see her now in my mind, traipsing up Snozzy's side aisle on a Saturday after she'd been to confession. On her head she wears a red-and-yellow scarf. She's heading for the Virgin Mary and the wrought-iron and copper candle holder, shaped like a heart, bright with burning candles. She even walks differently in church, humble, her head bowed. She slips a coin into the black box piled with drippings of candle wax, takes a candle, lights it from one of the others, and pushes it in a vacant holder. The holders are all clogged with wax drippings, green from the copper. Then she kneels down, bows her head, and prays for something, I don't know what—the souls of her departed mam and dad maybe, or the speedy recovery of one of her sisters, Molly or Nell or Kit, from whatever ails her, or for my dad that he not lose his job on the docks. Always the same performance. I've watched her do it for as long as I can remember.

I bet she lit a candle for me going away: that I come to no harm. That's her expression, "come to no harm." I hope she did light a candle. Not that I believe much in the power of candles to the Virgin, or any of that codswallop, but it does no harm to play it safe.

I can see my mam saying the rosary, the shiny green beads like emeralds, clasped to her chest. Or doing the stations of the cross, which is what Father Rigby hands out as a penance, after confession, to all the old biddies of the parish. With her dark eyes turned up and her lips moving in prayer, my mam looks like one of those holy pictures the nuns were always trying to flog to us for a

137

penny or twopence apiece to be kept in our prayer books to remind us of the lives of the saints.

Dad went to mass every Sunday, but that was about all. He didn't go in for all that rosary and candles and stations-of-the-cross stuff. Neither did I. It was different for men.

I tried to sleep, tried to make my mind a blank.

But I thought about the *Benares* in the middle of the ocean. Me on it, lying in my bunk, awake. Bleeker overhead, mumbling and muttering in his sleep. Charlie McCauley in his bed at home. Gordie Darwin somewhere in Derbyshire at his aunt and uncle's. Bren and Pat O'Dougherty somewhere in Ireland. All asleep except me.

Last summer, in the holidays, me and Bren and Charlie and Gordie sneaked out of our beds and met by the Regent Cinema in the blackout. It was Charlie's idea. There was a moon. It was one o'clock in the morning. The night was warm. We were pleased with ourselves that we'd managed to pull it off. I was a bit nervous, though, that my mam and dad might discover me missing. They would kill me.

"What shall we do now?" said Gordie.

"I dunno," said Bren.

"You know what I'd like to do?" said Charlie.

"What?" we said.

"Those dirty German spies have got their bedroom window open," said Charlie.

The Millers, a miserable old couple with no kids, lived at the top end of Baden Road. They always came out to

138

their backyard gate and yelled at us for making too much noise whenever we played Robin Hood or cowboys and Indians in the back jigger. Because the Millers—probably changed their name from Mueller, Charlie's dad said—had heavy foreign accents, we had decided early on in the war that they must be German spies.

Me and Bren and Gordie stood in the blacked-out street thinking about the possibilities of the Millers' open window, waiting to hear what Charlie had in mind. The white-painted markings on the lampposts and on the curbs glowed brightly in the moonlight.

"What I'd like to do," said Charlie, "is kidnap a cat and throw it in their bedroom window. If we're lucky, the cat might make enough noise to frighten the sauerkraut out of them."

"That's a good idea," said Bren. "A catnap."

"Let's find a cat," said Gordie.

"A tom," I said, "a big moggie"—the word we used for ugly, scarred cats—"that should do it."

We soon found the cat; there were millions of them in Baden Road. It was a big, heavy, battle-scarred moggie, but dopey and docile and soft as a brush. Charlie and Bren climbed up onto the Millers' backyard wall. Me and Gordie handed the cat up to them, and then we climbed up. Charlie handed Bren the cat while he stepped from the wall to the top of the air-raid shelter. Bren handed the cat across to him. We sat on the wall and waited to see how Charlie's scheme would work out.

Charlie got as close as he could to the open window, and tossed the cat into the bedroom.

139

The cat gave a savage screech as it landed somewhere inside the room. We heard the Millers screaming and yelling before we jumped to the ground and fled.

I sneaked back home. Nobody had missed me.

I grinned in my *Benares* bunk.

Catnap.

This wasn't helping me sleep.

Charlie was a joker.

Another time he slipped one of those big celluloid joke dog turds into the display window of Sayers Bakery, right in the middle of their cream and custard cakes, and then we hung about outside on Precky Road watching the disgusted phizogs of all the old biddies. We laughed.

For Charlie, windows were opportunities.

Bleeker started again with the cries and whimpers. I listened. He kept it up. I wondered if I should wake him. Nightmares were no fun. I knew.

Belfast kiss.

I didn't think I'd like to live in Belfast.

A Kildare kiss now, that'd be different. I was only little, but I remember Kildare, the place where I was born. Some of the rooms had no windows. I can't remember why not—something to do with taxes: the more windows, the higher the taxes, I think. I had nightmares sometimes. I used to think my unwindowed room was closing in on me, walls and ceiling breathing, and advancing slowly to crush me, and I'd wake up, crying. My mam used to come in to hold me and kiss me and tell me everything was all right. She'd light the lantern so I could see the room was normal.

Or an Achill kiss.

I liked Achill best, my dad's home; the summers there were slow and long.

I remember.

I throw myself down in the stubbled field and close my eyes while my dad and grandad swing their scythes at the last of the hay. The sun is hot.

Achill is the slowest place in the world. Even the speech is slow. Listening to a conversation between two Achill people is like listening to grass grow.

Con Begley, the postman, stops on his bicycle and peers over the hedge at my dad and grandad working. He starts filling his pipe. My dad and grandad see him and stroll over to the hedge. They nod at the postman, who nods back and continues filling his pipe. "It's the grand day," Con Begley says.

Grandad thinks for a while, and squints at the cloudless sky. Then he says, "It is."

The postman waits for a good while, and then he says to my dad, "Is it back ye are, then, Jack?"

Dad doesn't talk the slow way in Liverpool, only whenever he's home for a visit. So he waits for a bit, deliberating, and then he says, "It is, Con."

Con nods, and smokes his pipe, considering this answer, his gaze wandering out over the field.

"Just for the few weeks," Grandad adds when nobody has spoken for a good bit. Grandad has a bushy white mustache and light blue eyes, and he wears an old felt hat, stained with sweat and torn at the brim.

Con nods again.

I'm lying with the sun hot on my face, listening, my eyelids red and luminous.

Kissed by the sun.

After a long pause, Con says, "And is that the young feller now?"

Dad turns and takes a long slow look at me, seven or eight years old, in the grass, lying there with my eyes half-shut. "It is so," he finally admits.

Con puffs on his clay pipe. My dad and grandad test the edges of their scythe blades with their thumbs, and then stop and look at the field.

"The missus'll be with ye, then," Con says.

"Ah, she is," Dad says after a while.

Con, back on his bicycle, says, "Tell her hello from me, then, will ye." And off he goes.

"I will," my dad says to the hedge.

Bleeker had stopped whimpering.

I slipped into sleep with the sun on my eyelids and the sound of grass scythes swishing in my head.

FOURTEEN

Tuesday, September seventeenth. Our fifth day at sea. A dark day, with the air heavier than Lyle's treacle syrup.

In the morning the skies blackened and the rain started. I walked stiff-legged along a lurching deck behind Bleeker to breakfast. The steward pushed my chair in to the table, the way they always did with everyone, like we were royalty or something instead of a bunch of snotty-nosed kids. But I could eat nothing: the ship's motion was starting to make my stomach feel like the bubble in a spirit level.

Miss Fisher sat with the small kids at the other table.

I looked at Tony Curtin. Red nose. He looked rough. "You're a dirty fighter, Bleeker," he said, glaring.

"Don't start anything," I said to Curtin.

Bleeker looked at me, saying nothing.

Across the dining room, one of the women escorts was having trouble trying to calm a screaming kid.

Except for Fish 'n' Chips, everyone seemed to be testy. The small kids at the other table were acting up because of the heavy swaying motion of the ship, keeping Miss Fisher busy. Grice was in a silent mood. Patricia was busy with Elsie, cleaning the mess off the tablecloth where the ship's sway had helped her topple her milk. Theresa and Laura were not speaking to each other.

I drank some orange juice.

By afternoon the rain had stopped, but the thick air pressed down heavier than ever and the sky seemed damaged, black and bruised.

I took a shower, thinking it might make me feel better. Then I lay on my bunk trying to keep my mind off my stomach by rereading an old *Hotspur.*

The cabin door rattled open. Bleeker.

"Feeling green, are you, Jamie?"

That was a new one, calling me Jamie. I didn't like it. Boys never used first names unless they were friends. It was an unwritten law. Even the teachers at Snozzy's called the boys by their last names. Except when I was with my family and my pals, I felt more comfortable being called Monaghan. Did this mean Bleeker was starting to regard me as a pal? A friend?

"Leave me alone," I said.

"Didn't I tell you too many showers are bad for you. All that hot water and steam, and then going out in the cold. Best way to catch pneumonia. Be better for you to get in the fresh air, out on deck."

I searched his phizog to see if he was having me on, but his expression was serious, concerned.

144

I wasn't sure what to think about this new first-name sincerity.

He sat on the edge of my bunk and took off his shoes and socks. He had been leaving his shoes outside the door for the steward to clean. He now wore the cleanest, shiniest run-down, beat-up pair of string-laced black oxfords I'd ever seen.

My own shoes weren't that much better, to tell the truth, but at least I hadn't had the gall to leave them for someone else to clean for me.

"Best not to read while the ship's rolling," said Bleeker. He pulled out a long penknife. "Makes you feel worse." He levered out the blade with his thumbnail, and pointed it at me as if to emphasize his sincerity.

I looked at the knife, and then I looked at Bleeker. His face was hard to read because of the scowl and the bruises, but he had sounded friendly. We'd been thrown together, forced by the war to share a cabin, and he was feeling friendly. That was all. Besides, how did I know kids in Belfast didn't call each other by their first names? I didn't like him pointing his knife at me, though.

He turned away and began cutting his toenails with the knife.

"Do you have to do that in here? You think I want to walk about the cabin with your filthy toenails all over the floor!"

He went on cutting. "The cabin steward'll clean it up in the morning."

When he had finished, he pulled on his grubby gray socks and his shiny shoes, and put away his knife. He got

145

up. "Think I'll take a stroll on the deck." He grabbed the binoculars, reached the door, then turned slowly to look at me. "By the way, Jamie, I almost forgot to tell you. The Royal Navy escort left us last night."

"The navy ships have gone? How do you know?"

"I know."

"How do you know?"

"I got ears."

"But we're out of the danger zone, everyone says so."

Bleeker turned away and opened the cabin door.

"Bleeker?"

He stopped. "What?"

"I'll come with you. For that fresh air you said would be good for me."

We staggered together around the deck. It was difficult to stay upright. Neither of us spoke, but we bumped into each other several times. Bleeker had the binoculars resting on his chest, the strap around his neck. After a while we stopped at the rail on the top, on the boat deck. The wind whistled through the ropes. The ship's roll was so bad I couldn't see the horizon on the dip, only high, curving waves; and the black ocean joined seamlessly to black sky. I held on to the rail tightly with both hands. But I didn't feel sick, just cold, and scared to be so high on a ship that seemed frail in the uncertain and dangerous world of ocean and storm.

I looked sternward. The other ships were still there; I could see their shapes in the deepening gloom. We hadn't broken convoy.

I started to say something to Bleeker, but the wind

whipped the words away from my mouth and hurled them into the sea. I pounded his arm with my fist and pointed down to the lower deck. He turned away and moved down the steps to the promenade deck, where we found a sheltered spot behind one of the big ventilators.

I said, "Are you absolutely certain. About the navy escort, I mean?"

"I am."

"But we're still in the convoy, still going slow, same as before."

"So?"

"Seems funny, that's all."

"Are you two all right?" It was Fourth Officer Dunne, the one growing a mustache. He had a pink, plump face, and wore a navy blue duffel coat with brass buttons, the collar turned up around his chin.

"We're fine," I said, my hand on the ventilator for support.

"Bit rough up here," said Dunne. "Storm's getting worse. You'd better get below." He looked closely at Bleeker. "Seen that U-boat yet?" Jokey tone.

Bleeker shook his head. Because his arms were folded across his chest he was having trouble staying upright.

Dunne said, "We're not likely to see any U-boats around here. We're almost six hundred miles from home, and three hundred miles past the Northwestern Approaches, which is where the U-boats operate, off the Irish coast, waiting for the big convoys." He stopped and stared at Bleeker. "What's that you've got around your neck?"

"Huh?" Bleeker's eyes widened innocently.

"That strap." Dunne pointed.

Bleeker unfolded his arms, exposing the binoculars. "This? Just a pair of glasses I borrowed from—"

"From the wardroom. You stole them. They're mine. I've been searching for them everywhere. You little blighter, I've a good—"

Bleeker handed the binoculars over.

"I didn't steal them," said Bleeker. "I was going to put them back."

"You had no right to be in the wardroom in the first place. It's for ship's officers only."

"Chief," I said, trying to take his mind off Bleeker, "this is a fairly fast ship, isn't it?"

"If I catch you in there again!"

"Chief?"

He turned to me. "I'm not a chief. I'm Fourth Officer Dunne."

I said, "Mr. Dunne, what's the fastest we can do?"

"The *Benares* is exceptionally fast," said Dunne proudly. "She can do fifteen knots, sometimes better." He started to turn toward Bleeker again.

"What's a knot?" I said quickly.

"One nautical mile per hour," said Dunne. "A bit more than an ordinary mile. One point one five statute miles, to be exact."

"So how fast is fifteen knots?" said Bleeker.

Dunne turned back to Bleeker, the anger over the binoculars almost forgotten. "Oh, about seventeen miles an hour."

I looked out toward the front—the bow—of the ship just as it plunged down into a wall of water. It stayed down so long I thought it would never come back up. But then it slowly lifted. "What speed are we doing now?" I said.

Dunne frowned. "About eight knots or so, I think."

"But that's only half speed," said Bleeker.

"That's right," said Dunne. "We must all stay together, you see." He pulled at the peak of his cap, settling it more firmly on his head against a sudden gust of wind.

Bleeker looked suspicious. "Why do all the ships need to stay together?"

"It's a convoy," said Dunne. "For protection."

"But you just said there's no U-boats this far out," said Bleeker. "What do we need protection from?"

"Convoy stays together until the commodore gives orders to break."

I butted in. "Mr. Dunne, is that right about the navy escort leaving us?"

Dunne looked surprised. "Who told you that?"

"It's true, isn't it?" said Bleeker.

"As a matter of fact, yes. The navy left last night to meet with a Canadian convoy sailing to England." He shrugged. "But we're quite safe. Why don't you two stop worrying and go below where it's warm, and leave everything to us."

PLACE YOURSELF IN OUR HANDS.

Mr. Dunne pushed back the sleeve of his duffel coat to inspect an oversized chrome wristwatch with luminous green numbers. Long dark wrist hairs curled around the

149

silver expander watch strap. Then he shook his binoculars at Bleeker. "Stay out of the wardroom!" He hurried away along the deck into the wind.

We lurched drunkenly to our cabin. I thought about Bleeker and the binoculars.

My dad walloped me something fierce one time, called me a thief, after me and Bren pulled up some carrots from the Victory gardens in Thomas Lane. "There's nothing worse than a thief!" he yelled at me as he strapped me with his leather belt on my behind. "It's not a mortal sin," I cried. "It's worse than a mortal sin!" he yelled. "Once a thief, always a thief!" I didn't believe him that there was any sin worse than a mortal one, but I never stole after that.

I kicked off my shoes and threw myself onto my bunk. "You don't think anything's going to happen to us, do you, Bleeker?"

He sat on the floor with his back to the cabin door and pulled off his shoes. "I don't know, Jamie."

That "Jamie" again.

"Sailing on Friday the thirteenth. Do you really believe all that guff?"

He stared at the shoe in his hand, frowning. "Sometimes I do."

"But it's a stupid superstition. Friday the thirteenth is the same as any other date."

Bleeker hurled the shoe at the wall. "No it isn't, Jamie." He sounded quite certain. "I was born on Friday the thirteenth."

150

• • •

The noise and happiness of yesterday's festive party was one thing; today was something else: because of the rising storm, hardly anybody came to dinner. The blue-and-white-uniformed stewards stood about like dummies in Lewis's department store windows, swaying easily with the roll and pitch of the ship, hands lightly resting on the tops of the high-backed chairs, ready to lift them out for hungry diners.

Only Bleeker and his sister, and about six or seven other kids and four escorts—not Miss Fisher—were there to eat. Elsie sat alone, her doll on her knees. I watched Bleeker sit down beside his sister. They had the whole table to themselves. With their backs to me, they didn't know I was watching from the doorway. Bleeker took the doll, sat it on the edge of the table in front of Elsie, wiggled its arms and body, and spoke in his Dolly voice. Elsie laughed. Bleeker caused the doll to leap at Elsie's face and deliver kiss upon kiss to lips and cheeks and neck. Elsie writhed in ecstasy, her high childish laughter ringing across the almost empty dining room.

The storm was getting worse.

I slogged back to the cabin, heavy and tired, like I was made of lead, needing to lie down and close my eyes. I had the cabin to myself. I looked up at Bleeker's bunk, wondering what it would be like to sleep on the top. I changed the sheets and blankets and climbed up.

I relaxed in Bleeker's bunk feeling bold and defiant.

I was still wearing my day clothes, though, and my life

jacket: I liked the feeling of being bold and defiant, but there was no sense in taking chances. Bleeker's certainty about the U-boat was getting to me.

He would come in and see me in his bunk. He'd be angry. I lay there thinking, beginning to have second thoughts: perhaps it'd be wiser to play it safe; it wasn't too late to change the bedding back before Bleeker came barging in.

No! Why should I? Bleeker didn't scare me! Let him be angry! What did I care? If he woke me up, I'd tell him to sod off; it was my turn to sleep on the top.

I closed my eyes.

The ship pitched and rolled.

I fell asleep about nine o'clock. Bleeker wasn't back.

The torpedo struck the *Benares* and exploded at exactly ten o'clock.

FIFTEEN

Direct hit!

I was thrown out of the top bunk. My head struck something hard, and I fell to the floor, barely conscious.

This was it! The end! A direct hit, a German bomb—like the Trevor family, wiped out in a tiny fraction of a second.

But no! It couldn't be a German bomb. I remembered I was on the *Benares*. I could hear bells.

I tried to get up but couldn't move. I groped about blindly, head crazy and mad, ears destroyed with the clanging of bells.

Bleeker was yelling something at me, but my head and my ears were hurting and I could hear only the clang of the alarm bells.

"We've been hit!" yelled Bleeker in my ear, pulling at me.

"Hit?" I said stupidly.

"Get up, Jamie," said Bleeker. "Be quick. We got to hurry."

Why were the bells still clanging? Why was the cabin pitching and rolling? Why was there no light? How come Bleeker was pulling at my arm? I tried to stand, but fell back to the floor, weak and trembling. My head felt wet.

I could hear Bleeker grunting as he heaved, pulling me up, propping his shoulder under my arm.

"Try to walk, Jamie!"

I clung to Bleeker's neck, trying to walk, but my legs were too weak to support me.

"Let's go!" yelled Bleeker, half carrying, half dragging me out the cabin door. My head was bleeding; I could taste blood on my lips.

A rotten sulfur smell. Like bad eggs. I laughed shakily. "Stinky Corcoran must have farted," I murmured at Bleeker.

"We've been torpedoed!" Bleeker shouted at me.

My head became clearer. I willed strength to my legs and managed to stumble, taking some of the weight off Bleeker's shoulders.

"That's it, Jamie, try to walk. But hang on to me." We pressed forward against a river of moving bodies, pushing and shoving. The corridor was dark, and crowded. Shouts and cries of boys. High excited voices of Indian crewmen. Darkness. Lurching ship. Crush of bodies moving too slowly toward the exit.

I felt my arm beginning to slip from Bleeker's shoulders. He stopped to get a firmer grip on me, then staggered, grunting, along the tilted corridor.

Tilted.

The ship was sinking.

How much time was there before it sank and took us all down with it?

Wet stickiness in my eyes. Blood from my temple.

"Clear the doorway!" someone yelled.

"—German U-boat!"

"—torpedoed!"

"Torpedoed! Sinking! Get out!"

"Abandon ship!" Hysterical cry.

I was suffocating in the jammed corridor, in the acrid smell of sulfur, in the clanging of bells. I had to get outside onto the deck, into the air. Better to die in the open than to sink to the bottom of the sea trapped and buried alive inside the iron walls of a stinking ship. But my legs refused to obey me. I clung to Bleeker. He gripped the arm I had around his shoulder with one hand, and circled his other arm about my waist, dragging me, gasping with the effort. We were free of the crowd and staggering down the empty corridor, back toward the stern of the ship.

"I gotta find Elsie!" muttered Bleeker as he reeled drunkenly along the flooded corridor. I could feel my feet wet inside my shoes and socks. Like water to the roots of a dying plant, life gathered in my legs, and I tested their strength.

"Good lad, Jamie!" gasped Bleeker. "Try to walk!"

High jabbering voices. Girls. Some were crying. Damaged cabin doors, shattered timbers and debris, bits of cabin furniture, broken pipes blocked the way. We followed the sound of the girls' voices, clambering through and over the blockages, Bleeker pushing and pulling at me, lifting me, urging me on.

He paused at a splintered cabin door. "You in there, Worm?" he yelled.

I dragged at him. "We've got to get out!" I yelled in his ear.

He kicked the door open. The cabin was empty.

We stumbled blindly away along the tilted corridor, following the sounds of the crew and the girls into yet another blockage of pipes and timbers. Someone pushed into us and I almost fell from Bleeker's shoulders, but he grunted and hitched me up straight again.

A woman on the other side of the blockage called, "Get down on your knees and crawl through!"

The ship lurched. Bleeker lowered me to the flooded floor and I squirmed forward on knees and elbows, under the blockage, hoping the timbers wouldn't collapse and crush me. I could hear small kids crying up ahead. I felt like crying, too: all I could think about was being buried alive in the drowned ship. I wriggled desperately through the debris and slopping water, and then felt someone's hands on my arm, trying to help me up. I couldn't see who it was. I couldn't stand. A second pair of hands grabbed me. Bleeker.

I was led and helped over the doorsill onto the windy deck, where it seemed like daylight after the darkness of the passageways, and I sucked in a deep breath of stormy night air, relieved that I was not to be buried alive in the bowels of the ship.

The main deck was littered with broken glass and piping, and pieces of metal from the shattered and twisted rails.

There was a moon.

The wind howled.

I knew we were standing directly over the place where the torpedo had struck because the rail had been torn away, and the edges of the deck were twisted upward from the force of the explosion. I pictured the sea pouring into the jagged hole torn into the ship's side, claiming her, dragging her moaning and sighing slowly but surely down to the deep.

I clung to Bleeker. We stood there in a gale, unable to move. We were like the two statues of Jesus and St. Joseph, one each side of the altar in Snozzy's, their hands extended, frozen in a blessing since 1842, when the church was built.

PLACE YOURSELF . . .

We teetered on the edge of a high sloping cliff, with the rushing wind coming at us from behind and threatening to blow us off into the gaping wound far below.

The sulfur smell was stronger here. I wanted to be sick.

"Jamie! Come on!" Bleeker was the first to move, his shoulder under my arm again, dragging me away from the edge.

One of the women escorts, Mrs. Sanderson, was hanging on to a rail and directing everyone toward the stairway. I ordered my legs to move, and tried to take some of the weight off Bleeker as we followed the girls and the crew up the steps to the muster station on the promenade deck.

We were out of the wind. I felt stronger. Bleeker eased me down onto a couch.

The clock in the playroom showed ten minutes after ten.

Fully dressed in slacks and brown coat, the same ones she had worn when we came aboard, Fish 'n' Chips was busy checking life jackets and doing her Nurse Florence Nightingale on the injured. Patricia Richers was sitting, her eyes wide with fright. There was blood on her leg and on her hands.

Elsie ran to her brother. "Tom, we got 'sploded from our bunks." She was in her underpants and vest, bare feet, Dolly clasped to her thin chest.

Bleeker wiped a smear of blood from her cheek roughly with the back of his hand.

Elsie said, "We 'sploded out of bed. I fell on Patricia."

Miss Fisher knelt beside Patricia and tied a pad and bandage around her leg. One small kid had already been treated: she wore a bandage around her forehead. Fish 'n' Chips looked over at me. "I'll put a dressing on that head of yours, Jamie." She came over to me, carrying a first-aid kit. She cleaned my forehead. "The bleeding's stopped. I won't put a dressing on; the cut isn't deep." I remembered Beryl Oyler: ". . . our brave soldiers."

Most of the small kids were in their bare feet, hadn't

taken the time to dress. Under their life jackets they wore only pajamas or underclothing.

"Can I go back to my cabin for some clothes, Miss Fisher?" said one small kid.

"It's too late, Monica. We must get to the lifeboat right away. There are blankets in the boat." Miss Fisher's unhurried, confident manner calmed me a bit. I rolled off the couch and stood, legs stronger but my head still dizzy.

The bells clanged.

When Fish 'n' Chips was satisfied that we were all there, big kids and little ones, she signaled one of the other escorts, an older woman with a clipboard in her hand, then led the way out, leaning on the wall as she went. Patricia clung to her, limping badly. Elsie grabbed Patricia's pajama jacket and walked with her like Patricia was her mother.

The starboard was the weather side of the ship, the most exposed to the storm. When we moved out onto the deck, the storm tried to blow us back inside. I could see the crew moving about on the boat deck above, struggling to lower the lifeboat for boarding.

By now there was a small crowd of us at the muster station, half of them Indian crew, including Karam, the cabin steward. We held on to each other, backs to the gale.

The deck sloped: it was like standing on the side of a steep roof or on the Albany Street playground seesaw. The ship was going down at the stern and listing so badly toward port that our lifeboat swung inward, toward the ship, instead of out toward the sea. Elsie was calm. Every-

159

one was calm. Patricia was groaning; she leaned, one arm around Miss Fisher's waist.

The bells stopped. The ship's lights came on.

The PA crackled. "Prepare to abandon ship! Prepare to abandon ship!"

I stared around me: hurrying figures, the dark, moonlit outlines of our lifeboat swinging above our heads, the group of clinging, shivering kids, Fish 'n' Chips standing tall and straight, calmly holding the hands of two of the younger girls, like she might be waiting for the arrival of a Pier Head bus on Precky Road.

"Prepare to abandon ship!"

I looked down at the sloping deck beneath my feet.

The ship was sinking fast.

The deck officer yelled to his crew on the boat deck, "Stand by for lowering!

"Clear away the falls!

"Clear away the belly bands!"

Our boat was lowered jerkily while we all watched it in silence. I glanced at Bleeker to see if he was as scared as I was. The moonlight lit his face. He wasn't scowling. He was relaxed. Confronted by his Friday-the-thirteenth fears, he seemed relieved to be facing them at last.

SIXTEEN

The wind battered at the dangling lifeboat. It was big and heavy, and it swung crazily back and forth like a Big Nelly loose on its moorings. Officer Seeley barked orders at the crew, who were doing their best to hold it steady.

Boarding was tricky. Miss Fisher helped Patricia to a seat, climbed out again to supervise the boarding of the kids, and then climbed back in again. Elsie sat beside Patricia. Next was a couple of old geezers and an old biddy with a walking stick. Then the crew boarded, stewards mostly; I recognized a few of them. They looked scared.

We all sat holding on to something in the swinging boat—the side, a rope, the mast, anything to avoid being thrown out. Bleeker and I wrapped our legs around the mast, holding and riding it like it was a horse running in the Grand National at Aintree.

The crew had split into three groups, some in the stern and a few near the bow of the lifeboat. The third and largest group sat at the sides near the propeller handles. Officer Seeley sat up in front, yelling orders to someone above on the boat deck. Fish 'n' Chips sat in the center with several of the small kids, including the girl with the bandaged head.

I could see another lifeboat being launched ahead of us. Crowded with people, it leaned in over the deck instead of over the sea. The launch crew pushed, and it swung like a pendulum before being lowered over the side, past the upper deck, past the main deck, and down the steep side of the ship. The lowering was jerky: first the bow of the boat dropped, then the stern, then the bow again. The lifeboat thumped and walloped into the side of the ship as the wind attacked it. The bow dropped with another jerk. Then it stopped abruptly, catapulting a bunch of screaming people out from the front. They fell thirty or forty feet and disappeared in the black sea. Two or three of them were little kids.

"You see that, Jamie!" growled Bleeker, behind me. He yelled over to Elsie, "Drop Dolly and hold on with both hands!"

I clung grimly to the horizontal mast, stomach churning, heart hammering like a big circus drum.

It was our turn next. I felt the lifeboat drop suddenly, then stop, then plunge down just like the other boat, the ropes twisting and jamming because of the way we were leaning in toward the listing ship. It took all my strength to hang on. The terrified screams of the kids merged with the shriek of the wind as the stern of the boat came to an abrupt stop, still swinging from side to side, and threw a knot of people out of our boat into the waves that were battering the side of the ship far below.

I looked down in horror at the boiling sea, but there was nothing I could do but glue myself to the mast like a limpet to a rock. I couldn't see any of the people, not a single one. One minute they were sitting in the boat, and the next second they were gone. Snatched. As if they'd been plucked out by furious Neptune and dragged down under the ocean. My mind was dragged down into the broil with them. I felt myself choking for air.

This was it. I was about to die. Forgive me, Jesus, for all my sins. The short act of contrition. Saved from hell by seven words.

I looked down again. Only the spume and the hammering waves.

The boat shuddered and screamed against the side of the ship. I tried to figure who'd been thrown out. Three of the girls were missing. And two of the Indians. I closed my eyes, trying hard not to think of what was below, a hell of pounding water instead of fire, remembering faces instead. Three girls gone. Theresa. One of them was Theresa. The boat shuddered. And Laura. And the little one with the bandaged head—couldn't remember her name. What about Karam? Had he gone, too? Too scared to release my grip on the mast, I turned my head around as much as I could, searching for Karam, and glimpsed him behind me, clinging and terrified.

The lifeboat dropped again, more steadily this time, but, because of the heavy list, scraping and bumping, shuddering and shaking down the side of the sinking ship. The final drop went too fast, bow first, and we crashed hard down on the water at an angle, and were immediately flooded and hurled up against the iron side of the *Benares*. Several more Indians were tossed out. One of them was Karam. Shifting my grip from the mast to the side of the boat, I leaned over, ready to grab him, but he was under the boat, trapped between the lifeboat and the side of the ship. That was the last I saw of him.

Some of the other crewmen had grabbed oars and were futilely trying to push the boat away from the ship. Seeley was barking orders at them, but the wind and noise of the waves crashing against the ship tore the words away. One of the oars splintered and snapped.

"Man the Fleming gear!" yelled Seeley to the crew. But they'd already started turning the handles of the propeller gear, five of them on each side of the boat.

"Cast the sea anchor!" Seeley shouted from high in the bow of the boat.

A crewman stood and hurled out a big bucket-shaped thing on the end of a cable.

As the ten crewmen bent to their task at the propeller gear, our flooded lifeboat slowly pulled away from the ship's side and headed into waves higher than a house that tossed the lifeboat up and then plunged it down. I thought of the roller coaster at Blackpool. This was ten times worse. The boat took on more water. Though still sitting on the seat, I was up to my chest in it. The boat was flooded to the gunwales: I wondered why it hadn't sunk.

I was terrified.

Seeley yelled for everyone to throw their weight over to the side to keep the flooded boat from capsizing.

As we lurched crazily about, the boat charged up a high wave, poised for an instant on the crest, and I saw the *Benares,* all her lights blazing, stern down, rearing her head into the air and starting a slow slide. We were still close enough to be sucked down with her, I thought. Seeley barked out orders. The men worked the propeller as hard as they could.

There was a loud explosion and flash of light.

Down into the valley.

And up. I could see another ship off in the distance burning—oil tanker probably—hit by a torpedo. Distress flares, yellow, white, and red, splashed the night sky like fireworks.

Up again, the waves battering over the side of the boat, me and Bleeker throwing ourselves into them to balance the boat. The flames from the burning ship painted our faces red. The thick oil fumes carried on the wind made us cough.

The *Benares* wasn't burning. Her bows lifted high out of the water and, lights still blazing, she slipped into the black ocean in a quick clean slide. I heard a muffled explosion as the sea flooded her generators and the lights went out.

We all watched.

And she was gone. To the bottom of the sea. Swallowed by the ocean. With nothing to show where she had been, except the moonlit swells.

165

We had abandoned her not a minute too soon.

I hung on desperately, expecting to be sucked under with her. Instead, a mess of waves came rolling and battering at our waterlogged lifeboat and swept Patricia, Elsie, and another girl overboard.

Miss Fisher screamed.

The shock of seeing the three girls swept away out of the lifeboat so easily and quickly caused everyone else to freeze.

Except Bleeker.

As Miss Fisher screamed, Bleeker whirled from where he was trying to help balance the boat, and threw himself into the boiling water after the three girls.

I stared, unable to move. Someone was screaming, one of the girls. I could see no sign of the four lost kids. Then, as the lifeboat climbed out of the trough, I saw orange life jackets bobbing about on the water.

"Stick out the oar!" someone roared.

Bleeker seized his sister's life jacket, and hauled her back toward the boat. The other two girls, Patricia and Monica, were clinging to each other, far from the boat.

"Teng!" Seeley yelled at one of the crewmen. "Try to bring her round!"

Teng, tall and wiry, was the man on the rudder, but all he could do was try to keep the flooded boat steady so we didn't capsize.

"Hold her there!" yelled Seeley.

Several of us rushed to the side, splashing through the water, ready to grab Elsie. Hands reached out to pull the pair aboard. Bleeker pushed Elsie up out of the water toward the flooded boat. Seeley and I snatched at her and missed. Then I caught her by the arm and pulled her in, and collapsed backward into the boat, Elsie clasped to my chest.

I looked back for Bleeker, but he'd gone, snatched away by a curling wave.

The lifeboat dipped into a trough. When it came up again, there was no sign of Bleeker or the two girls.

SEVENTEEN

Silence except for the booming sounds of sea and wind.

I could see several boats in the fitful moonlight, all flooded like ours, and riding so low in the water that only their bows and sterns were showing. It was impossible to count how many there were because of our deep drops into wave troughs when all I could see was a wall of water.

Over in the distance, the other ship was still burning, the sea around it a bright circle of flaming oil.

Seeley yelled, "Teng! Start bailing!"

Teng yelled in his own language, and some of the Indian crewmen began to bail water from the boat. They eventually gave up when the water poured back in as fast as it went out.

The moon disappeared behind the clouds. I couldn't see anyone's phizog. I was seated with Elsie in my lap; the water came up to our chests. It was the buoyancy tanks, I finally figured, that were keeping the boat afloat.

I looked for the burning ship. It had disappeared. Now there was only darkness.

We waited for the rescue ship to come.

My eyes soon became accustomed to the darkness and I could make out the shapes of the people in the boat.

Elsie was shivering. I put my school cap on her head and pulled it down about her ears. *Semper Fidelis*. Then I undid the green rope from around my waist and tied Elsie to me, looping the rope around her middle so she couldn't be swept away.

"Stay awake, Wendy," said Miss Fisher to a small kid clasped to her chest. "The rescue ship will be here soon."

Up ahead of me an old woman was crying.

"Mrs. Zimmerman!" said Miss Fisher, sharpish like. "Could you hold on to Jill?" She pointed to a little girl who was having trouble clinging to the gunwale.

The old woman splashed over to the other side of the boat and gathered the girl up into her arms, then sat down again, massaging the girl's arms and legs and murmuring soothingly to her.

The sea was calmer now; the waves became less terrifying. The moon stayed hidden behind the clouds.

"Blankets, Teng!" shouted Seeley.

Teng groped under the water and began to pull wet blankets from the submerged lockers. He passed them around. I took one and wrapped it around myself and Elsie.

"Margaret! Ursula!" yelled Miss Fisher at two small girls who were falling asleep. "Wake up!" She reached over, grabbed one of them by the life jacket, and shook it, calling, "Climb up to the front with Mr. Seeley."

Seeley waded down from the bow to help, lifting them one at a time into the bow, wrapping them in a blanket, and then holding their skinny bodies in his arms against the marauding currents. Their small white phizogs were like pools of light in the darkness.

It was very cold. Colder than a witch's tit, Charlie would say. I clenched my teeth and felt my jaw trembling. There was no feeling in my legs. Why was the rescue ship taking so bleeding long to find us?

We waited.

I was thirsty.

The Indian crewmen mumbled prayers.

Teng, fumbling in the underwater lockers, found a bottle of rum and some corned beef and ruined biscuits. I took a swig of rum. It burned and warmed me. I made Elsie sip a little of it, but she coughed it back up. I gave her some more, and this time she swallowed it down.

Nobody wanted the food.

"Is there water?" groaned an old man.

Teng searched, but there was no water.

The rum had made me thirstier than ever. I wanted to sleep, but I put my eyes to work searching the darkness around me. Nothing, no lights, no ships. There'd been many ships in the convoy: where were they?

It rained and hailed, cold and stinging. I hunched my shoulders and hugged Elsie tight to my chest.

We waited.

Elsie's head fell forward. I slapped her face, but she didn't respond.

"Wake up!" I slapped her again and pinched her arm. Her eyes opened.

"You've got to stay awake, Elsie!"

The water swirled about our chests.

The rain stopped, and after a while the moon showed its phizog again.

Miss Fisher started yelling at the turbaned Indians, who were slumped over, asleep or in a coma. "Wake up!" she cried.

Her voice sounded cracked.

One of the Indians slipped sideways into the water and didn't come up. Teng grabbed him, but the man was dead. I don't know how I knew; I just knew. I'd never seen a dead person before. He looked fine, like he was sleeping. Teng let him go and the dead man went under, then bobbed up again just as a wave came sweeping over the boat and washed him overboard. I watched sleepily. It was like he was just setting off to the corner shop for a bag of crisps or a bar of chocolate and would be back in a jiffy.

Seeley was saying a prayer for the man: I heard the words, ". . . works of the Lord."

The old lady wailed, "She's gone!" She rocked Jill violently back and forth. "She's gone!"

Seeley said quietly, "Push her over the side." He started with the prayers again. "They that go down to the sea in ships . . . see the works of the Lord, and his wonders in the deep."

The old lady, ignoring Seeley's order, rocked and cried and clasped the limp body to her breast, the small blue face barely above the water.

The moon disappeared.

I forced myself to think of other things, like the only fight I ever had at school, 'cept it wasn't a proper fight because John Hurley simply walked up to me and gave me a punch on the nose and I stood staring at him, the blood running down my face. I was so surprised that it didn't occur to me to punch him back. I went home all bloody, and my mam was mad at me. I discovered later that Hurley had stolen a stick of chalk and a package of cigarettes from Miss Delaney's desk, and she found out and gave him three after-school detentions. Someone told Hurley that it was me who snitched on him, which wasn't true.

I tried to think of more stuff, but couldn't think of very much except people's faces: my mam smiling, dark hair, brown eyes, pale skin; my dad intent, arguing about the Irish Anti-Partition League with Matt O'Dougherty; Madeleine's shining face when she sang; Bren's quiff falling into his eyes; Charlie's grimace as he pushed his glasses up on his nose; Gordie's slow grin.

Seeley was praying again. An Indian. ". . . abide with Him in heaven, we commit his body to the deep. May he rest in . . ."

I stopped listening.

The night dragged on in stiff, cold, huddled silence.

The cold was killing us.

"Stay awake," said Miss Fisher weakly.

I wanted to sleep. The cold was the worst, but the next most awful thing was that everything was salty—the water, my face, lips, throat. I was crusted all over with thick salt and I couldn't put my tongue out, couldn't move my lips, or hardly get my eyes open if once I closed them, the eyelids sticking shut with gummy brine. It was like I was being buried in salt a mile thick.

Water. I needed a drink of water.

Moonlight again.

Jill's blue face.

Nobody spoke. Except for the Indians mumbling their prayers, and the slap of the waves across the submerged boat, it was quiet. The wind had died down; the waves became less terrifying.

The rescue ship had to be out there in the dark, searching for us.

The moon disappeared.

We waited.

And waited. The longest night of my life.

Rain and hail again, deadly cold.

Trying to stay awake.

At one time during the night, the water around my thighs was pleasantly warm from my pee, but then the cold waves came in again.

I don't remember much of what happened after that.

All I remember is the terrible cold and Elsie wearing my cap and her skinny body tied to me with my rope and the universe being made of salt.

Then, finally, daylight, dawn the yellow color of turnip, and everything crusted with salt like a thick frost, and the

173

sea like Miss O'Hara's blackboard, dusty chalk and slate, wiped clean. Empty.

Father Rigby was wrong about hell being everlasting fire: hell is made of salt and wet and cold, terrible, terrible cold.

I remember dreams.

I'm with my mam and dad and Bleeker under the stairs and the Jerries drop high explosives all around us. *Thump! Thwack! Thump! Thwack! Thump! Thwack!* We're huddling together, hands over our ears, waiting for that direct hit, the one that will take us off. "Drink," says a voice, and I suck on a straw or tube and drink, waiting for the direct hit.

I'm cold.

Another dream. Madeleine sings "Kelly, the Boy from Kilane." The Bleekers start fighting next door. *Thump! Thwack! Thump! Thwack!* Bleeker staggers in and collapses on the floor in front of Madeleine. Bleeker's heart is bleeding like the one in the picture of the Sacred Heart Mam keeps on her bedroom wall. "Sing 'The Irish Soldier Boy' for me," Bleeker gasps to Madeleine, and then he's swept away in a huge curling wave—*Thump! Thwack!*—before Madeleine can open her mouth to save him.

Another dream. I'm flying high over the waves with my hands outstretched for wings. I look down, and the sea is strewn with flowers, orange and blue. I fly down low to take a closer look and see that they're not flowers at all but dead kids bobbing about in the waves in life jackets, their faces blue like petals. One of them is wearing a man's dirty blue pinstripe jacket.

"Drink," says the voice again.

Thump! Thwack! Thump! Thwack!

I awake to the noise of engines. A voice says, "Drink."

I'm colder than a polar bear's bollocks. "What day is it?"

"Thursday, chum. Drink."

I suck water till it dribbles down my chin. We were torpedoed Tuesday night. I want to ask about Elsie and Bleeker, but instead I fall asleep again.

The next time I wake, I say, "Where am I?" The engine sounds like a familiar piece of music. *Thump! Thwack! Thump! Thwack!*

A man's voice says cheerfully, "You're safe, son."

"What day is it?"

"Friday."

I try to move. My arms feel like they're around Elsie. I look down. No Elsie. "Where is she?"

"Take it easy, lad. Here, take another drink."

Bleeker, what about Bleeker? I try to sit up.

"Easy there, chum!"

Suspended in the air in a ship's engine room. In a hammock. I try again to sit up, but have lost the use of all my muscles, like I've been switched off at the mains. I try moving my toes but can't feel them.

A phizog squinting down at me. A sailor. Smells of tobacco. I think of my dad. I try to speak, but all that comes out is a croak.

"Take it easy, laddie. You're going home."

Home.

I close my eyes and sleep.

EIGHTEEN

When I saw them I cried.

I couldn't help it.

My mam clung to me and wouldn't let me go.

Rows of beds. I was in a hospital ward.

Mam cried.

My ribs hurt, and my shoulder; tears stung my lips.

She finally sat down and I looked at my worried dad, that slanting line furrowing his forehead, nervous fingers turning his cap around and around in his lap.

"How are you, Jamie?"

"Fine, Dad, thanks . . . very . . . much." Hoarse, aching from my mam's arms, tongue swollen, mouth tender and sore, I wiped my face of tears, hoping nobody else, boys, in the ward had seen me cry.

"Ah, Jamie!" My mam gripped my arm through the blanket, and then rose again, peering at my sore mouth. My hand flew up to touch the swelling there. Lips chapped and crusty with dried blood. "Careful," said my mam. "Ye don't want to start the bleeding again."

Sunshine edged through high windows down at the end of the ward and splashed yellow onto the polished brown linoleum floor. The ward's green walls cast a sickly light over my mam and dad's long faces. The ward was like an ant colony, people walking up and down, the sound of a wireless: Vera Lynn singing "We'll Meet Again." Ha!

I pushed my back up against the hard iron bed rail. I felt weak. I was wearing a loose, white nightgown. I wriggled to pull up the gown and examined my side where it was sore. Bruises like faded inkblots. I ran my fingers up, feeling the shoulder's tenderness, and then remembered . . .

Bleeker!

I scanned the double row of beds.

And Elsie. Where was Elsie?

"Rest easy, Jamie," said my mam, who was trying to examine my ribs for herself. "There's no sense—"

"What 'bout Bleeker?" The words blubbery through thick lips.

My dad said, "He's in Special Observation."

"Bleek . . ."

My dad gave a long sigh. "Ah! It's in critical condition he is; that's what they say. Touch and go. The girl, Elsie, is across the hall; she's fine. Sleeping mostly, like yourself, but she's fine."

Bleeker alive! Ah! Didn't I know he'd make it. I forgot my sore lips and aching ribs and lay back. My mam's

178

hands fussed with the pillow behind my back. I closed my eyes.

Special Observation was where they kept the snuff-it-any-minute patients, I knew that much from the time Gordie's dad had a heart attack, but Bleeker was here and he was alive.

I must have sighed or groaned or something because my mam said, "Ah! Ye'll soon be home, Jamie, love."

Home.

"Where are we?"

"Glasgow General," said my dad.

Scotland.

"You can't send me away again, you just can't!" I felt the blood rush to my face. "I won't go!"

Mam gave a low groan. Dad said, "No, Jamie, not again. If Hitler drops one on us, we'll go together, the three of us."

"There's no place safe," said my mam. "We'll take our chances as a family, so we will. Ah! God was good to bring ye back to us, Jamie."

I could see that Mam was about to cry again. I said, "Help me up."

I suddenly needed to go real bad. They had been waking me often to make me drink, though it wasn't really waking, unwaking more like; and there was a cold bottle they shoved into the bed at me.

I slid out of bed, my legs so weak I almost fell. My mam tried to catch me, but the nurse saw me and hurried over and took me by the arm. Light-headed, and afraid I would wet myself, I lurched unsteadily, knees held tight together. The nurse was young and reminded me of Miss Fisher. Where was Fish 'n' Chips? My mam was talking to the nurse, saying she would go with me, but the nurse said for her to sit and wait.

I peed like a racehorse, as Charlie would say, and then, leaning on the basin, looked at myself in the mirror over the washbasin. My face was whiter than a plate of tripe, but the worst thing was the eyes and lips: eyes the yellow-brown color of dog turds, and lips swollen and scaly with bits of skin and dried blood. God! I looked like I'd crawled out of a shithouse!

When I got back I noticed a brown paper shopping bag beside the bed. I collapsed on the bed and pulled the bag closer. Clothing. Mine. The blazer was ruined, shrunken and stained by the sea, the blue of badge and motto no longer royal, the gold *Semper Fidelis* now only a pale yellow. Blue trousers cleaned and folded, but I could see they'd fit me no more. Jersey and ruined shoes at the bottom, no cap. I remembered I'd put the cap on Elsie's head. Silk parachute rope, the green leached out of it.

At the bottom of the bag, my wallet, the once black leather now gray and shriveled. I looked inside and then handed it to my dad.

He took the wallet in his hands and opened it. The ten-bob note was still there where he'd put it. He looked at it for the longest time without saying anything. Then he folded the wallet closed and put it back in the bag.

My mam took my hands and held them tight. Her fingers were ice-cold.

．．．

Sirens in the dark. After a while they stop and I hear faint stirrings, people breathing, someone talking in a low voice. I move my head on the pillow. Faint light down at the end of the ward from the nurses' room.

Bleeker.

I swing my legs over the side of the bed and slide down the few inches to the floor. The bed is higher than what I'm used to. The white hospital gown comes down to my ankles almost. Like a ghost dressed for haunting, I shuffle down the center of the ward, ignoring the sleepers in the shadows.

I tiptoe past the nurses' room. The hallway is dark, with only a night-light casting a faint orange glow over each doorway; my heart feels like I've been running. I stop to catch my breath. Then, hugging the wall, I move on down the hallway and peer at the signs on the doors.

OBSERVATION ROOM.

I look behind me along the hallway. Nobody. I push the door open and slide in. I'm in a dark room. There's a viewing window and, on the other side of it, another room with a night-light bright enough for me to see Bleeker's mam kneeling beside a high bed, praying. She's wearing a blue head scarf, the spitting image of the Virgin Mary in the thirteenth station of the cross up on Snozzy's wall next to the confessional.

Bleeker, sleeping or dead, white, thin like a twig.

She gets up off her knees and sits. She's been crying; face shiny wet. She pushes Bleeker's hair off his forehead

181

and lightly touches his face with the backs of her fingers, gently, like he's made of glass.

I turn and get out of there sharpish.

Morning. I wander about. Everything's green in this place: walls, doors, even the orderlies' uniforms. I wonder if they pee green piss.

I also wonder why I haven't seen Miss Fisher, or Curtin, or Grice.

I see Grice. I think it's Grice, but it's hard to be certain. He's asleep. People, visitors, his parents probably and some others, sit around his bed.

A man in a dark suit goes around the ward asking questions and writing in his notebook with a fountain pen.

I haven't looked at all the beds, but already I'm exhausted. I go back to my own bed and close my eyes.

Daylight. Mrs. Bleeker leaning over my bed, peering at me. She gives me a fright. I stare at her red face framed by frizzy brown hair leaping out of her blue head scarf, no Virgin Mary now. Seeing me awake, she clutches me, crushing my sore shoulder. When she lets me go, I can see her eyes are tired, like she hasn't slept in a long time.

"How's Bleek—Tom?" I can hardly speak, my lips are so swollen.

"Holding his own." Mrs. Bleeker's red face almost collapses. "He's fighting, isn't he, Brian?" She turns to the man beside her.

Bleeker's dad is a little man, nervous and twitchy, with

a thin face, wispy brown hair, and pale blue eyes. He grips my hand and pumps it up and down several times, almost crushing the bones and causing my bruised shoulder to ache. "Jamie, we appreciate what you did. The girl, the escort . . ."

"Miss Fisher," says Mrs. Bleeker, moving to separate our two hands. "Go easy with the boy . . ."

Mr. Bleeker lets my hand drop. ". . . Miss Fisher said you took good care of Elsie."

"We'll never be able to thank you enough," says Mrs. Bleeker, pushing her husband behind her and away from me.

"Can I go and see how . . . Tom is?"

"They'll not let you in," says Mrs. Bleeker. "But Elsie asks for Jamie all the time. Are you able to come across the hall to see her?"

I slowly swing my feet onto the floor. She takes me by the arm, and we go down the floor together, Mr. Bleeker following, and across the hall into the next ward. I'm shuffling like an old geezer, but my legs feel stronger, though ribs and shoulder are still sore.

Elsie seems lost in the big bed. Her eyes brighten when she sees me. "Hello, Jamie," she whispers.

"Hello, Elsie." She tries to smile through swollen lips as I touch her pale cheek with my fingers.

"Tom's here."

"I know."

"Dolly's gone."

"Yes."

• • •

Night. A faint light in the nurses' room.

I throw back the covers and let my feet find the cool floor. The light from the nurses' room falls on my gown, or shroud it looks like, and I'm haunting the place. If anyone bumps into me in the dark, they'll piss their pants.

I creep past the nurses' room, out the door, along the hallway, and into Special Ob.

The tiny night-light glows in the darkness. The room on the other side of the observation window is empty except for the bed. I go into the room, to the bed, and look down on Bleeker. He is lying on his back, straight and still like he's in a coffin. He could be dead. I move closer to the bed and trip on Mrs. Bleeker's purse on the floor beside the chair.

"Bleeker!" I say in a loud whisper.

Nothing.

I lean down closer to his face. "Bleeker! It's me, Monaghan."

I watch his face. Was that a faint movement under the eyelids? I can't be sure. I call his name again, but he doesn't stir.

A toilet flushes. Bleeker's mam.

I'm out of there. I close the door quietly behind me and creep back to bed.

In the morning the man with the notebook and fountain pen came and sat by my bed. He had gray hair and wore glasses and reminded me of Mr. Hale. He said he was Mr. Montgomery from the Ministry of Shipping.

He already knew my name. He asked me a few questions about how I was feeling and whether I'd been injured when the torpedo struck, or when everyone was climbing into the boats.

I shook my head.

He asked me questions about how the Indian crew behaved during the evacuation of the ship, but I didn't answer. His eyes glinted behind the glasses. I didn't like him. He wasn't a bit like Mr. Hale after all. I turned my head away from him and stared at the wall.

He asked me more questions, and I told him to sod off.

My mam and dad came in, and the man got up and left.

They must have wheeled Tom Bleeker into the ward late in the afternoon. I had dozed off, and when I awoke, he was there, down at the end near the nurses' station. I knew it was him because his mam was there. I got out of bed carefully, still a bit light-headed, and shuffled down to the end.

It was him. He was asleep, so pale he looked like a corpse. His mam looked terrible. She smiled at me. I stood there a long time watching until the nurse saw me and ordered me back to bed and made me drink more water.

Fish 'n' Chips was there after all. She came to see me before she left. "At last I find you awake, Jamie." She gave a wan smile. "Every time I come by to see you, you're snoring your head off."

We talked.

"I'm so pleased about Tom," she said. "He's out of danger."

Out of danger. I liked the sound of that.

"It's a miracle how he managed to hang on to the bottom of a capsized lifeboat for so long," said Miss Fisher. "The sailors who picked him up said it took all their strength to pry his fingers off the keel."

She talked about the others. The old people didn't make it. Most of the little kids had died of the cold.

"Patricia?"

She shook her head.

"Laura and Theresa? Little Monica?"

She shook her head again.

We were silent for a while.

"A few never woke up. They died in their sleep on the *Hurricane.*"

"There was a hurricane?"

"The name of the rescue ship," said Miss Fisher, "HMS *Hurricane.*"

I asked her if she would be going back to the escort job on another ship. "There will be no more, Jamie, not after . . . not after this."

She wrote down her Gloucestershire address and telephone number. "Come and see me sometime, Jamie," she said, trying for another smile, face thin, lips chapped.

"Goodbye, miss," I said. "And thanks."

"Take care, Jamie." And she was gone.

I forgot to ask about Officer Seeley.

Grice, up and about, came to sit on the edge of my bed

after my mam and dad had gone to get something to eat.

"Your old mate was touch and go for a while there," said Grice.

"Bleeker? He'll be all right," I said. "Did Curtin make it?"

Grice nodded. " 'Is mom come in a private h'ambulance and took 'im 'ome to London." He grinned. "I'm off first thing in the morning. What about you?"

"Sometime tomorrow, I think."

We headed down to Bleeker's bed.

He was awake.

"Hello, Bleeker," said Grice.

Bleeker stared, rose slightly, and tried to speak, but then fell back on his pillow.

We moved closer. Bleeker closed his eyes.

There were sirens in the night, and for a while I thought I was home in my own bed, and I expected my mam to come yelling at me to get down to the bunk under the stairs.

NINETEEN

Tom Bleeker is up and about.

He's . . . different.

His eyes glitter startlingly blue in a face that's thinner, with all the bruising gone, and except for the chapped and swollen lips, it's as though a night and a day in the cold sea has healed him. Changed him.

I'm sitting on my bed, reading one of the comics my mam brought, a *Wizard*, when he walks over, moving differently, without the usual swagger. Then he stands and looks at me, quiet like, no leers or winks, no scowl, just those intense blue eyes weighing me calmly.

"Hello, Jamie."

"Hello, Bleeker."

I look him in the eye and he just stands there looking back, not acting tough or anything. I make room for him on my bed and he sits on the edge. "You feeling okay?" I ask him.

"Not bad." He grimaces slightly. "I don't think I want to arm-wrestle, though."

"No, me neither." We stare at each other, noticing the changes. His fingers are all stiff and bent, like claws. "What happened to your fingers?" I say, remembering too late what Miss Fisher had said about him clinging to the keel of a capsized lifeboat.

He holds his hands up in front of his face and looks at them. "The doc says they'll straighten out."

There's silence for a while, and then I say, "I go home today. What about you?"

"They said tomorrow, but my mam put her foot down and said we go back today. It's because my da just got a job in the munitions factory."

"That's good."

"Yeah."

"Elsie's okay."

"Yeah."

"You glad to be going home?"

"Didn't want to go away in the first place."

"Me neither." I try not to stare. He's wearing a shapeless shroud, like mine, but I can't get over the change in his appearance. "I s'pose you'd rather go back to Belfast."

He shakes his head. "No."

"You like Snozzy's?"

"Yeah."

We watch the young nurse go by, the pretty one. She smiles at us.

I say to Bleeker, "Smashing legs."

189

"Yeah."

"You want a comic?"

"Okay."

"Help yourself." I move over to make more room on the bed.

With claw fingers he chooses a *Hotspur* and sits beside me with his back against the bed rail and we read for a while and then he falls asleep.

A man came to the hospital from the Admiralty. The other man, the one who had been asking questions, Mr. Montgomery, left yesterday. The Admiralty man also went around asking questions. He asked me if I was all right, and I said yes. He gave my dad some papers and travel vouchers.

We ride home on the train, Monaghans and Bleekers together. Nobody says much. Bleeker sleeps most of the way. Then we all squeeze into a taxi at Lime Street Station, and when we get out at Baden Road, the O'Doughertys and all the neighbors are there, and most of the population of Old Swan it looks like, all gathered under a big WELCOME sign stretched the whole way across the street.

They all cheer. It's brilliant. Elsie enjoys it the most if you ask me. Tom Bleeker doesn't look too happy, though, probably because the journey down from Scotland did him in; he looks awful. But he can't avoid talking to the reporters from the *Echo* and the *Daily Mail*. We have to stand together and have pictures taken. The reporters already know about him saving his sister's life.

They persuade him to stand with his arm around Elsie, but they can't make him smile.

Charlie's there. He looks smashing with his wild red hair temporarily tamed with brush and Brilliantine.

"You hear anything from Gordie?" I say.

"No. Still milking cows in Derbyshire far as I know."

"What about Bren?"

"His mam says he's fine. You gonna be back at school tomorrow?"

"You betcha."

"You feel okay?" says Charlie.

"I'm fine." My legs feel stronger and my mouth is okay.

"Everyone's been asking about youse all, you and the Bleekers."

"Yeah?"

"Yeah."

"Been any air raids?"

Charlie shrugs. "Some. But we're getting used to them." He grins. "It's smashin' having you back, Jamie."

When everyone has gone, we go into my house, Charlie and his mam and dad and the O'Doughertys, too.

Dad takes me up to my room. The charred furniture has all been thrown out. He shows me how he's fixing it. It isn't finished, but the holes in the floor and roof have been repaired and the walls have been stripped and cleaned. "I told himself I'd fix it all if he supplied the wood and materials."

I look at him. "Himself? You talked to the landlord!"

My dad shrugs. "No, not the landlord, but the rent man, Paddy Malone."

I laugh. "It looks great. But there's still a lot wants doing."

"Ah, there is."

"I'll give you a hand."

"A hand'd be welcome sure enough."

We go back downstairs and we all have the tea Madeleine has ready for us, and some Cadbury's chocolate biscuits she used her own ration coupons on. Afterward she sings, "The Harp That Once Thro' Tara's Halls" and "The Irish Soldier Boy," her ruddy face shining and her hair like burnished copper, and we all sit and listen, and my mam cries, and it's good to be home.

I look at Bleeker. He's pale and tired, but he's sipping Madeleine's tea and listening to her sing. His mam comes over and sits beside him and slides her hand along the chair so it's touching his. Madeleine finishes "Irish Soldier Boy" and everyone claps.

Mam and Mrs. Bleeker sit with tears running down their faces.

The bombers come that same night.

Dad has laid a plywood floor in the shelter—part of the landlord's "supplies." And there's a small table and a paraffin lamp. With chairs and stools, it's almost comfortable. Better than sleeping under the stairs. I love it. What I mean is: I love being in it. It's home even if it is overcrowded.

Dad and Mr. O'Dougherty and Mr. Bleeker sit on the outside step, smoking Woodies and talking, ready to jump in if things get rough. I sit on the plywood floor with Tom, our backs to the wall. The tarp door is propped half open and I can see the bursting flares and the Big Nellies. Elsie, on her mam's lap, has a new doll, a long soft thing in blue gingham. Mrs. Bleeker is knitting a brown jersey for Tom. Mrs. O'Dougherty in her nice coat, the one with the fur collar, is telling Mrs. Bleeker about her sister Nancy in Edenderry, and Madeleine is showing my mam something in the *Woman's Weekly*.

I don't even care if we get a direct hit. Why worry? I look at Tom. He's got his eyes closed, relaxed, not saying anything.

I hear the guns going and the bombs falling, but they're far off. Jerry is getting more accurate, my dad says. "It's the docks and the aircraft factory in Speke they're after."

"I'll make the cup of tea," says my mam, and gets up and feathers her fingers through my hair as she goes by on her way to the house. Madeleine goes with her, the two of them chattering together like a pair of Irish magpies.

Mr. Hale is out in the hallway ringing the bell the way he always does at the end of the day.

It's good to be here listening to it.

Instead of ringing or rattling or clanging like most bells, our bell booms along the hallways and up the stairs to the second floor of the school where I am, and today it sounds like it's booming for me and the Bleekers.

I came to school half expecting to be called a sissy for

running away—that's what they did to Charlie when he came back from evacuation last year. But it wasn't like that; everyone asked questions, treating me and Tom like heroes. There was a party for us in the classroom; Mr. Hale came. That's never happened before.

Miss O'Hara's bulletin boards are covered all over with stuff about the sinking. There's newspaper pictures of the ship and some of the survivors, and some of the ones who died, and headlines from the *Liverpool Echo* and the *Daily Mirror*: "83 CHILDREN DIE AS HUNS SINK LINER IN STORM."

The bell has stopped, but it's still booming in my ears as I heave myself up and join Charlie McCauley and Tom Bleeker and all the other kids in the familiar four o'clock rush for freedom. Classroom doors fly open and hundreds of feet pound down the wooden stairs the way they always do; then they thunder out the door, down Snozzy's worn granite steps, and into the warm, waiting sunshine.

Tom Bleeker's wearing a Royal Navy sweater, "HMS *Hurricane*," which a sailor must have given him on the ship; it almost fits and he looks good. Different. He's got almost all his old energy back. And he hasn't scowled at anyone all day, not once. He leaps down the steps, me and Charlie close behind him, and he's whooping and yelling, so we do the same, we whoop and yell, and Tom grabs Charlie's school cap off his head and jams it down on his own, and we cheer.

Elsie's waiting at the gate.

"Move yer legs, worm!" I yell at her.

And we make for the Albany Street playground, skipping and running, and hooting, and Charlie swoops and grabs his hat back off Tom's head and whops him one on the backside with it.

"Let's go!" yells Tom.

So we go.

This work of fiction is based on the true story of the sinking of the passenger liner *City of Benares*. I am indebted to Ralph Barker and his *Children of the* Benares: *A War Crime and Its Victims* (London: Methuen, 1987).

According to Barker's account, there were ninety government-sponsored (CORB) evacuee children on the ship and ten additional children who had been privately paid for, four of whom did not survive. The final total of CORB children who died after the sinking of the *Benares* was seventy-seven, and not eighty-three, as stated in the newspapers of the day: it was discovered eight days after the sinking that a further six children (and a group of adults) had survived in a crowded but unflooded lifeboat that had managed to make it almost all the way to Ireland, a distance of more than six hundred miles, before being spotted by a British aircraft and rescued.

The two torpedoed ships, *Benares* and *Marina,* were abandoned by the rest of the convoy: not one of the other ships searched for survivors, but made away from the scene as fast as they could. The original destroyer escort, HMS *Winchelsea,* was not ordered back for rescue duty. The rescue vessel, HMS *Hurricane,* took eighteen hours to reach the scene. It is certain that had there been a rescue ship nearer at hand, there would have been many more survivors.

It seems almost certain also that if the *Benares* had left the "convoy" and sailed at her normal (faster) speed after the destroyer escort left, then the U-boat would never have caught her.

From the point of view of the German U-boat, *U-48*, the *Benares* was the flagship, the biggest and most important ship in the convoy.

The total number of people who lost their lives, passengers and crew, in the *City of Benares* was 256; the total number of survivors, 150. Only nineteen out of the one hundred children aboard the ship survived.

The characters in this story are fictional and are not meant to represent anyone, living or dead.